UNTIL I BREAK

KARA BIETZ

ALBERT WHITMAN AND COMPANY
CHICAGO, ILLINOIS

For Steve, who has always believed I could

Library of Congress Cataloging-in-Publication
data is on file with the publisher.

Text copyright © 2016 by Kara Bietz
Published in 2016 by Albert Whitman & Company
ISBN 978-0-8075-7438-6 (hardcover)
ISBN 978-0-8075-7440-9 (paperback)

Printed in the United States of America
10 9 8 7 6 5 4 3 2 1 BP 20 19 18 17 16

Hand lettering by Jordan Kost
Design by Ellen Kokontis

For more information about Albert Whitman & Company,
visit our web site at www.albertwhitman.com.

TODAY
1:02 p.m.

The barrel of the gun is warm against my temple.

I can hear the frantic *fwump-fwump-fwump* of my heart slamming against my ribs in the chaotic hallway.

A tiny voice inside is fighting its way up my throat. *No. No, no, no*, it's saying. The sound never makes it past my teeth.

Loud, quick footfalls echo through the marble hallway. The sun streams through the thick-paned windows and glints off the trophy case, throwing golden stripes of light across the green lockers.

Ace's breathing is labored. His eyes are wide and wild.

I sink to the floor.

Darkness.

MAY
Twelve Months Before

My tie is choking me, my shoes are pinching my toes, and we've only been here for five minutes. Mom is fidgeting next to me, looking over the heads of everyone in the ballroom and wringing her hands. I can see her pulse thrumming on the side of her neck.

"You okay?" I ask her, nudging her foot with mine.

She nods too quickly, like a bobblehead doll. "Yeah. Yeah, I'm okay. It's just...crowded," she says with a one-sided smile. "Are you nervous?"

"Crowds don't make me nervous, Mom. Plus, this is mostly people we know," I answer, pulling at my collar. I swallow my own feelings about tonight while a thousand things go unspoken between us.

"That's not what I meant, and you know it," she says. "This is a big night for you."

I curl my toes in my too-tight shoes and look at the napkin in front of me. It's folded in the shape of a swan.

"So are you nervous?" Mom asks again. I notice that she isn't fidgeting quite as much as she was when we first got here. Her eyes aren't darting around the room like they were before either.

The tension in my own chest releases, and I smile at her. "I don't think so. I guess I'm trying not to think about it."

She pats my knee. "I'm proud of you," she says close to my ear. "No matter what the outcome."

I look at the banner over the podium at the front of the room. EASTHAVEN DAILY CHRONICLE STUDENT ATHLETE AWARDS is spelled out in block letters. A whole bunch of square-shaped glass awards are on a table behind the podium. When I got the letter two weeks ago that I had been nominated for Student Athlete of the Year, Mom hung it on the refrigerator with four magnets instead of one.

"See that? All of your hard work has paid off! So proud of you, Sammy," she said.

The response card for the awards banquet sat on the counter until the day before it was due to be mailed back. There were four blank lines under the heading "Attending."

Mom scribbled her name on the second line and my name on the third line and handed the card to me. "Take this," she said, barely disguising the edge in her voice.

I glanced down at it, fully aware of the empty line at the top. A knot formed in my chest, and I tried to swallow it down. Little reminders that Dad was gone snuck up on us like that. Most of the time we could sense it coming and avoid a direct hit, but sometimes it smacked Mom and me right where it hurt.

I held the card in my hand and wanted to say something to her. *It's okay. We're going to be all right. We've made it through worse. I'm proud of you for being strong about this.*

"I'll go put this in the mailbox," I said, running my fingers over that blank line at the top.

Mom and I find our table in the ballroom, and I'm about to pick up the place card near us to see whom we'll be sharing a table with when I hear a high-pitched voice carry across the room.

"Well, look who it is," the voice singsongs.

"Susan! How nice to see you here," Mom says, standing up and giving the woman a quick hug.

Shit.

Susan Quinn is our next-door neighbor. Her son, Ace, and I, we're not exactly buds. In trying to keep Mom calm, I had almost managed to forget that Ace would be here tonight too.

"Ms. North, Samuel, what luck that we're sitting together!" I hear behind Mrs. Quinn.

Of course we're sitting together. Of course we are. *Double shit.*

"Hi, Ace," I murmur, holding my hand out. He shakes it, squeezing my knuckles and looking right in my eye. He doesn't smile.

"I didn't know you were nominated for anything, Sam. Congratulations!" Mr. Quinn shakes my hand and claps me on the shoulder. "Ace here is getting a passing-yards leader award for football, and he's going to be the next Student Athlete of the Year. Isn't that right, Ace?"

Ace's eyes twitch ever so slightly, but he turns on a giant smile. "That's right. What about you, Sam?" he asks.

"Point guard assists for basketball. And I'm up for Student Athlete too."

The table falls quiet for a beat longer than is comfortable. Finally Mr. Quinn clears his throat. "Well, good luck to both of you, then," he says, raising his water glass and quickly bringing it to his lips. I see the muscles in his jaw flex as he shoots a pointed look at his son.

Ace avoids his father's cold glance.

Mrs. Quinn and my mother chatter about some new app my mother has been using. Mr. Quinn is full engrossed in his phone, frantically typing a message with his thumbs. Ace sits next to me, his leg bouncing up and down.

"I guess I'm a shoo-in, then," he whispers.

I swallow hard but don't answer.

"Cat got your tongue, Samantha?"

I bite the inside of my cheek to keep from answering. It's

not worth it. The longer I can ignore him, the better. Like a toddler, he eventually gets bored and turns his attention elsewhere.

He smirks. "If you're my competition, I'll be sure to win. Faggot," he whispers.

I can't pinpoint when the trouble began with Ace. My mom has pictures of the two of us playing together as preschoolers, when the nickname Ace hadn't yet stuck and everyone still called him Dean Junior. There are tons of those pictures of us together and smiling, drawing in the street with chalk, digging in the sand at the neighborhood beach. I don't feel like I know that smiling kid next to me in those pictures.

I do know this Ace. The asshole with the smart mouth. The slimy son of a bitch who is sure to turn the charm up to eleven when adults are listening.

I remember him in kindergarten, pouring water on my chair and telling the class that I had wet my pants.

And in fifth grade, when he stole my jeans from my PE locker, forcing me to wear tight PE shorts for the rest of the day in mid-February. Later he drew penises all over those jeans with a red Sharpie. The next day he wrote my name inside the waistband and shoved them in the lost-and-found box at school.

And I remember Ace when we were twelve. A rock forms in my throat at the thought.

The ballroom is getting crowded, and almost all of the

tables are full of high-school athletes from around the area and their parents.

"Whose name is on the place card over there, Susan?" my mom asks, taking a bite of the salad that has just been put down in front of us.

"It says Keaton," Susan says, holding it up for the rest of us to see. "Oh, Mary and Neil's daughter, I'm sure. That cute little sweetheart you boys used to play with when you were little? I can never remember her name. What is it again, Ace?"

"Marnie," I answer before Ace can.

Ace turns to face me, and his smile widens slowly. "Yes, Marnie," he says, kicking my shoe under the table. His face never loses the smile.

"Where's your father, Jenny? Shouldn't he be here?" Susan asks Mom, looking around the ballroom.

"He's up front with the rest of the coaches," my mom answers, pointing out Grandpa Carl at the big, long table at the front of the room. "He's so proud of Sam," she adds.

"Of course he is! As he should be," Ace says, another slick smile pulling on his stupid face. The heel of his shoe digs into my foot so hard I feel the knuckles of my toes crack.

"I know he's proud of you too, Ace. His star quarterback," my mom says, smiling at Ace and patting his hand across the table.

Ace makes his best "aw, shucks" face, then glances quickly at his dad with wide eyes. Mr. Quinn is scrolling through emails on his phone. Ace's lips tighten, and he looks down at his lap.

From my spot at the table, I see Marnie come through the ballroom doors in a purple dress, her hair pulled away from her face. She's knitting her eyebrows, and worry lines appear on her forehead. She pulls at the hem of her dress, fidgets with her watch, and looks around the ballroom slowly. She spots our table and waves to her parents behind her. I see her take a deep breath and plaster a big smile on her face before she walks over, all bubbles and sunshine. Her parents follow.

I stand up and pull her chair out for her, as well as her mom's. Ace's top lip curls in a sneer as he watches me.

"Mr. and Mrs. Keaton, it's so nice to see you again. And Marnie, you're looking as beautiful as ever," Ace says, standing up from the table and shaking hands with the Keatons. When Marnie reaches her hand out for Ace to shake, he brings it to his lips and kisses it instead. Marnie giggles.

"Sorry we're running a little late," Mr. Keaton says, his eyes darting over to his wife.

Mrs. Keaton lowers her eyes and wipes her brow. "Yes, sorry," she mumbles.

"You didn't miss anything important. Just a limp salad," my mom says, and everyone laughs. I'm happy to see that she's relaxing a little bit.

I glance at Marnie, and she gives me a little nod. "Hi," she mouths with a soft smile. Her eyes dance in the light.

"Hi," I mouth back, my stomach fluttery.

Ace digs the heel of his shoe into my ankle hard enough to leave a bruise.

"Headed out on any hunting trips this summer, Dean?" Marnie's dad asks Mr. Quinn.

"Ace and I have got a little trip to Louisiana planned...a little handgun hog hunting," he says. "My boy's got a real eye with a .357."

"Is that right?" Mr. Keaton says, his eyebrows rising in admiration.

"Yes, sir. I never miss," Ace says.

"How about you, Neil? Got plans this season?"

Mr. Keaton slowly shakes his head. "No time anymore. Though I have to admit I do miss it."

"You ought to come with us to Louisiana," Mr. Quinn says. "Just like the old days when the kids were younger."

"It's definitely something to think about," Mr. Keaton answers. "Though I don't know that I could convince Marnie to haul out her old camouflage and come with me anymore," he adds, laughing.

"No way," she says, shaking her head emphatically. "Barbaric," she says with a disgusted look on her face.

"Look at the three of you sitting there in your fancy outfits," Mrs. Quinn says. "I've got to get a picture of this. Scoot your chair closer to Sam, Ace. Marnie, you stand behind the boys. Lean in and smile, now!" She points her phone at us and beams. "Seems like last week you were headed to kindergarten together."

Marnie makes her way back to her seat, but Ace doesn't scoot his chair away from mine. I move my chair a few inches over, but Ace just scoots closer again.

"Where you going, buddy?" he whispers.

A man has made his way to the podium and is clearing his throat into the microphone.

"I'd like to take a moment to welcome you all to the *Easthaven Daily Chronicle* Student Athlete Awards," he says, stepping back from the microphone and clapping to the side. The audience takes the cue, and we all politely clap too. Mr. Quinn lets out a loud wolf whistle.

"I am William Lynch, the editor in chief of the *Chronicle*. Here in Easthaven, we are fortunate to have three top-notch high schools. Whitlow, Gadsden, and Broadmeadow High Schools have produced a staggering number of outstanding college and professional athletes as well as great thinkers..."

Mr. Lynch drones on and on while we scrape our dessert plates. I eye the number of awards on the table behind the podium. There have to be fifty of them. The biggest one, Student Athlete of the Year, will be the last one they hand out. I lean back in my chair and adjust my tie a little bit. I contemplate taking off my shoes under the table, but decide that's probably a horrible idea.

I glance at Marnie again. She's turned her seat around to

watch the speech, but I can still see a bit of the side of her face. Soft cheek, eyelash, and the corner of her mouth. My eyes trace the curve of her neck down to her shoulder. She fidgets with her watch again, her fingers twisting the dial back and forth, back and forth.

"Keep dreaming, Samantha," Ace whispers in my ear.

I narrow my eyes at him.

"Marnie Keaton. There's no fucking way," he says, snorting.

I sit up straighter in my chair and try not to look at Ace or the back of Marnie's head. Her neck. The way the skin on her shoulder pinches just slightly under the tug of her dress strap. The delicate brown curls that dance around her temple.

"She'd never fuck you, dickless," Ace says.

"Shut up, Ace," I mumble, mostly to myself.

The awards seem to drag on and on. Most Improved, Best Defense, Leading Scorer. One by one, kids approach the stage and then have their picture taken with Mr. Lynch while holding their glass award. Football is first, and Ace brings his small glass trophy back to our table to a chorus of oohs and aahs. Marnie is the next to win—a school spirit award. Ace gives her a standing ovation and a loud whistle. She rolls her eyes at him, and her cheeks turn red. She gives him a playful backhand as she sits back down.

"Nice job," I mouth when she looks at me.

"Thank you," she mouths back, the smooth skin above her dimples burning a bright pink.

Basketball is the last sport to be awarded, and by the time I get my small glass trophy, everyone has had just about enough of sitting in this ballroom. There are no more oohs and aahs.

"Good job, Sammy," my mom says, reaching across the table to squeeze my hand. "I can put it in my purse if you'd like," she adds.

I hand it to her and she quietly mouths "Proud of you," while everyone at the table chatters.

"There's just one more award, ladies and gentlemen. The Scholar Athlete Award," Mr. Lynch announces.

I sit up straighter in my chair, clenching my fists against my pant legs. My knee bounces, and I can't make it stop. I swallow a few times, hoping to make my heart stop slamming against my ribs.

It's only an award, Sam. It's only an award. It means nothing. Slow down. Breathe.

"What's up with you, North? You look like you have to take a crap," Ace says in my ear.

I ignore him and try to focus on breathing slowly. My mom reaches over to grab my hand and gives it a squeeze. "I'm proud of you either way, Sammy," she whispers.

"The *Easthaven Daily Chronicle* Scholar Athlete Award celebrates excellence in the classroom, as well as excellence in the competition arena," Mr. Lynch says.

It has to be me. Please let it be me.

"This year's scholar athlete is a young man who plays two

sports and has still managed to earn straight A's in all academic subjects."

Is it me? How many of the other nominees have straight A's?

"He will be a senior at Broadmeadow High School next year, and we are anxious to see what his final year of high school athletics will bring. He's a key member of both the football and basketball teams, and I am pleased to announce that this year's Scholar Athlete Award goes to Mr. Sam North. Come on up here, Sam!"

The ballroom erupts again in applause, but my ears tune it out. I turn to my mom and point to my chest. "Me?" I mouth.

Mom wipes a tear and nods. I stand and look toward the stage, where Mr. Lynch is waiting with my award.

I did it. I won.

I turn and look down at Ace sitting next to me, a huge smile pulling on my cheeks. His mouth is set in a straight line, his right hand squeezed into a fist. He looks up at me and shakes his head slowly. The straight line of his lips becomes a snarl.

"Congratulations, Sam!" Marnie comes around the table and hugs me. I try to ignore the dagger eyes I'm getting from Ace. Her hair brushes my nose. Wildflowers and spearmint. She squeezes my arm and pats my back. I touch the soft spot on her shoulder where her dress strap has pulled on her skin and made it pink.

A pat means you're just friends, wanker. That's what my best friend, JC, says. *If she rubs your back when you hug her, well…that's a different story. A pat equals total friend zone.*

"Go, silly! Go get your award!" she says, laughing and tapping my shoulder again.

Right. My award. The tips of my fingers tingle where they touched her skin.

I walk up the stairs, my mouth still stretched into a way-too-wide grin, and only trip a little. I don't think anyone notices. I shake hands with Mr. Lynch before accepting my trophy and certificate. I look back into the crowd and find Marnie again, clapping with her hands over her head.

Grandpa is standing up and clapping loudly. He has his version of a smile on his face, which can easily be mistaken for a sneer, but I can tell he's proud. He's nodding his head approvingly and clapping louder than anyone else in the ballroom. There are flashes in my face as the photographer takes my picture and the audience grows quieter.

I glance at the front row from the corner of my eye and see Grandpa still clapping for me. A few rows back, I see my whole table standing and clapping for me. Ace Quinn is clapping too, but really slowly. *Clap, stop. Clap, stop.* He's staring at me with his jaw set and his eyes unblinking.

Sore loser. Screw him, this is all mine.

I catch Ace's eye and start to smile. He looks toward Marnie for just a split second and then back at me.

"Fuck you," he mouths.

"That concludes our program, folks. Please join us in the room next door for coffee and dancing," Mr. Lynch announces into the microphone.

The guests start to file into the banquet hall lobby, and I see Mr. Quinn take Ace's arm and pull him toward the door. He gestures toward the stage and shakes his head slowly. Ace says something to him, and Mr. Quinn stops in his tracks. He stares at Ace, juts his chin out, and puts his hands on his hips, leaning toward his son. Ace puts his head down and shoves his hands into his pockets. Mr. Quinn leaves the ballroom, shaking his head and pulling his cell phone out of his pocket. My mom motions to the lobby, and I wave at her to let her know I'll see her out there. Mr. Lynch asks me to say a few words to the sports reporter and then asks for a few more pictures for the article.

I can't find Mom in the lobby after the pictures are over, but I really have to use the bathroom. Tucking the large trophy under my arm, I swing the heavy wooden door open with my foot.

Ace stands at the sink with an athlete from another school. Both are washing their hands.

"Congrats, Sam," the other guy says.

"Thanks, man," I say to him on my way into a stall.

While I'm in there, I hear the heavy door open and close.

I finish what I'm doing and exit the stall.

Ace is leaning against the sink, arms folded.

"Congratulations, Samantha," he says.

I set the trophy next to me on the sink ledge while I wash my hands.

"Thanks," I say, fully expecting a verbal beatdown from Ace. I ready myself with my two favorite comebacks: shut up and fuck off.

"Wipe that shit-eating grin off your face," he says, taking a step closer to me at the sink.

I don't say anything. Something about this Ace feels off. I'm used to listening to his shit, but this feels like more. He's breathing through his nose like a bull ready to charge.

"I'm talking to you, North," he says, getting right up next to me. His eyes bounce across my face, and the muscles in his jaw flex as he grinds his teeth.

He grabs the award from the sink and turns it over in his hands. "I can't fucking believe it was you," he says. "Do you know what my dad said to me after you won? He said, 'How could you let him beat you?' Unfuckingbelievable."

I have a flash of being twelve years old again, with Ace standing over me.

You're not twelve years old anymore, Sam. You're bigger. Stronger. Smarter than he is.

"Hey, give it back now," I say, swallowing hard.

"How badly do you want it? You think you deserve it more than I do, pussy?"

"Give it back, Ace. I'm serious." I approach him, but something in his eyes makes me afraid to get too close. His nostrils are flaring and his eyes are wild. Beads of sweat form along his hairline.

"Give it back, Ace. I'm serious," he parrots back to me in a whiny lisp.

"Come on, man. Don't do this." My voice cracks a little bit.

"Or what? You'll cry?" Ace laughs and backs away from me. "Or you'll tell Grandpa on me? Is that it? I won your precious grampy his first state championship, didn't I? Who is he going to believe? His star quarterback? Or his pussy, benchwarming QB2? You know who he likes better." Ace holds the trophy high over his head, but he moves closer to me.

I try to grab for my award, but I'm not nearly close enough to get it from his hands. I stumble a little in my attempt and Ace laughs.

"I should have this. A real football player deserves it, don't you think? You're certainly not a real football player, and basketball is for pussies. Maybe I should just take it," he says, bringing it down closer and running his finger over my name etched into the glass.

"Come on, Ace." I swallow as much fear as will fit down my throat. I don't like how wild his eyes look. "It has my name on it," I say.

Ace only backs up a step or two, and his face turns even stormier. "It has your name on it? Well, then, by all means, you should have it back," he says. His jaw flexing and his eyes shining, he holds it out to me.

I watch him for a minute, and the dread in my gut tightens. His eyes narrow as the award balances in the palm of his hand in the space between us.

I make a move to take it from him, and he suddenly raises his arm up over his head and slams the award down hard onto the marble floor. Thousands of tiny shards of glass scatter all over.

I watch the tiny pieces tumble across the floor without breathing. Ace kicks a few bigger chunks toward me with his toe.

"You're so clumsy. I can't believe you dropped it. They never should have given it to you," he says, stepping around me and leaving the bathroom.

3

TODAY
2:32 p.m.

Pain radiates from every inch of my skin. Throbbing in my jaw. Searing in my forehead. A dull ache in my chest.

"How did a kid like you end up here?" the guy with the tie asks.

He drops a manila folder on the small table and sits down in the chair across from me with a sigh. He's got deep wrinkles around his eyes and a sad puppy-dog mouth. He's like a basset hound in a rumpled dress shirt.

I turn my head to look at him. The slight motion produces an ache so deep and black that I let out a little choking noise.

"I'm Michael. I work here. Can we talk about this?" he asks, his voice soft and measured.

I look down at my wrists. Miniscule specks of blood kiss

my skin.

"If you talk to me, we will get this all cleared up. Your mom is waiting…"

I snap my head up and meet his eyes. Fresh throbs travel to my temple, and I immediately regret moving so quickly.

"That's it. Hi," Michael says again, a hint of a smile touching his cheeks.

"Who is with my mom?" I manage to croak.

"She's…she's alone, I think," Michael says, cocking his head to the side and narrowing his eyes. "One thing at a time, though, Sam. Let's talk about what happened today."

She's alone. She shouldn't be alone. The muscles in my stomach pull taut, and the pain traveling across my ribs intensifies.

"She shouldn't be alone," I say.

"If we can talk about this, you'll be able to go to her," Michael says, his voice quiet but insistent.

My eyelids feel heavy. She's alone out there, waiting for me. Is she pacing? Balling her fists? Curled up under a chair? Don't they understand that she can't be alone?

"Sam?" Michael leans forward on his elbows, his voice barely above a whisper.

I look down at my hands again. A new stinging pain reaches up from the soles of my feet and grabs my throat.

"Don't leave her alone," I croak, the heavy feeling in my throat choking me.

I pull my eyebrows together and look right at him. When he

swallows, his tie bobs around his throat like it's tied too tight. I wonder if it hurts.

"What if I have someone check on her? Would that be okay?" Michael rises from his chair, not bothering to wait for an answer from me.

He pokes his head out the door and mumbles to someone I can't see. When he comes back inside, he lowers his large frame back into the chair with a smile.

I look at him, expecting him to say something about Mom. *Is she safe? Is she okay? How many times did you ask her if she's okay? It takes at least three times before she admits that something's not okay. If you only ask her twice, she's not going to tell you the truth.*

My mouth can't form the words.

Michael flips a page in his notebook and nods at me. "It's all good," he says.

I try to imagine that she's okay. That Grandpa is with her. That whatever is happening beyond the heavy door won't be something that sends her into a tailspin.

I'm okay, Mom. Okay, okay, okay. I say the word in my head over and over. Maybe if I concentrate hard enough, she'll feel it. She'll know I'm okay, and she won't fall apart.

"Can you tell me about your dad?" Michael asks, chewing on his pen cap.

I try to shift my feet, but I can't move. I feel like I am covered in lead weights.

"How long has it been just you and your mom?" Michael says.

Fresh waves of pain travel up my back.

"Can I have some water?" I ask.

"We can do that," he says, pouring from the pink plastic pitcher by his side into a Styrofoam cup.

He holds it to my lips, and I take a long sip.

The pounding in my forehead lessens.

"Okay?" he asks, putting the cup down beside me.

I nod.

He stares at me, his pen at the ready.

I want him to ask that question again. About me and my mom.

"You've got to talk to me, Sam," he says.

The pounding starts again.

"Tell me about your grandpa. How long has he lived with you and your mom?"

"Almost a year," I say.

All I want to do is close my eyes and make this room disappear.

"Do you and your grandpa...Are you close?"

Close? I don't even know what the word means anymore.

"I don't really know," I say.

"Did you do things together? Is he someone you trust? Someone you'd go to if you needed help?"

No. "We did things together," I say. *Things he wanted to do,* I don't say.

"What kinds of things?"

I shrug. "He was my football coach," I say to my lap.

"Anything else?"

I close my eyes and see him loading the black gun cases into the back of his truck every month. "The range," I say.

"The range?"

"He took me to the gun range every month," I say.

Michael loosens his tie. Dark green with tiny black dogs all over it.

4

JUNE
Eleven Months Before

School ended shortly after the Student Athlete Awards Ceremony. The next day, Ace and his father left for their annual boar-hunting trip. Ace never mentioned what happened in the bathroom that night. Not that I gave him a chance. Whenever I saw him coming, I'd quickly change course and walk down a different hallway.

I was operating under the assumption that Ace would go on his hunting trip and maybe forget whatever major problem he suddenly had with me. Or maybe he'd go away on his trip and fully satisfy whatever sick need he had for causing pain and suffering by killing a bunch of wild pigs. Maybe then he'd leave me the hell alone. Maybe if I could just stay out of his way, fly under the radar a little, I'd be out of the line of fire.

I never told anyone what really happened to my award that night either. I stuck with Ace's story that I was clumsy and dropped it in the bathroom. Grandpa gave me an earful about being more responsible, and I just stood there and took it while Ace watched, a satisfied smirk on his face. The next day Grandpa made me email the *Easthaven Daily Chronicle*. I had to lie and say that I accidentally dropped my trophy and ask if it would be possible to get a replacement. I never heard back from editors at the paper. It's probably one of those emails that is sent around for everyone to read and have a good chuckle. "Hey, did you hear about the kid that dropped his trophy and then asked for a new one?"

Part of me doesn't care so much about the trophy. I can't think back to that night without my thoughts immediately turning to Ace.

There was something about him that night, something I haven't been able to shake. It was his face. The way his eyes narrowed on me like all he wanted was to destroy me. Sure, he had always been a grade A asshole. Sure, I had dealt with his finger in my back for years while he smiled and played nice for everyone watching, but this was so different.

I chalked it up to Ace being a sore loser at first. And don't think I didn't relish the fact that he couldn't stand to see me win something. But his voice. The way his nostrils flared when he looked at me. It was enough to make me strategically plan my routes to classes to avoid him for the last few days of school.

When I saw his father's SUV pull out of their driveway

on the last day of school, loaded down with guns and gear, I breathed a huge sigh of relief. I was convinced that as soon as Ace went on his little boar-killing spree, he'd go back to being just a normal asshole. I could handle a normal asshole.

* * *

My best friend, JC, and I work at the community-center sports camp together. We met there way back in third grade and have spent every summer there since.

When I get to work during the second full week of camp, there are bunches of brightly colored balloons tied everywhere. Some of them say "Good-bye" or "We Will Miss You" in glittery script.

"What's going on?" I ask JC when I get to the staff room. I pull my basketball shoes from the top shelf of my locker and crumple the list of my campers' names into my pocket.

"Tuck is leaving," JC says, shoving his bag in his locker.

"The football guy? How come?" I ask, putting my whistle around my neck. Working the summer sports camps at the community center is a pretty sought-after job. Not many people leave if they're lucky enough to be hired. Especially not after only two weeks of work.

"I think he's moving out of state," JC says. "I wasn't really listening. The new football guy is supposed to be here late this afternoon. Wanna take bets on who it is?"

"No way I'm betting you anything. But what are you thinking?"

"Gotta be someone from Broadmeadow."

"Why do you think that?" I ask as we leave the staff room together and head out to meet the camper buses.

He shrugs. "The community-college football team has already started their two-a-days. No one from there is going to give up a practice to come play football with little kids all day long. Gadsden and Whitlow High both have private summer sports programs for kids at their schools. And there aren't many schmucks around here that would take a crappy day-camp football coach job for the summer. A Broadmeadow football player could at least put it on his college apps."

"My grandpa didn't say anything to me...so whoever it is didn't use him as a reference to get the job," I say to JC.

JC shrugs. "I'm telling you...I'd bet my entire paycheck that it's someone from Broadmeadow."

"As long as it's not—"

"Don't even say it. I know, I know, as long as it's not Ace." JC rolls his eyes at me.

I lower my head. JC doesn't see it. No one does. And mentioning it makes me sound like a whiny pussy.

We walk away from the locker room and out the glass front doors to wait for the buses. "I don't like the guy either, but I don't, like, piss fire about it like you do. He's a jackass. So what? Ignore that shit. Most of that part of the football crowd is jackasses. Why should I hate Ace more than I hate the others?"

He's not waiting for an answer. And I'm not going to give him one.

"Have you seen Marnie since school ended?" he asks.

"Here and there," I say, thankful for the change of subject. "Not a lot. Not enough."

"You need to move on that, bro," JC says, knocking his knuckles into my back.

"These things take time," I say, laughing.

"If you don't make a move soon, I'm gonna get the two of you alone in a room somewhere and tell her myself! You've been drooling over Marnie Keaton since the fifth grade, man. Shit or get off the pot." JC laughs.

"It just never seems like the right time," I say.

"Hey," he says, grabbing both of my shoulders. "Make the time. Seriously."

"Alright, alright. By the Fourth of July. Swear," I say, holding my hands up.

"That's like three weeks from now!"

I shrug. "What if she laughs at me or something? I don't want to be humiliated."

"Seriously, Sam. You never know what she's going to say unless you ask."

"Okay, okay! I will. I promise."

"No chickening out," JC says.

"Scout's honor," I tell him.

The buses start to pull up, and it's JC's and my job to make sure the kids get off the bus safely and move into the building without killing each other or running away. On the first day of camp, JC and I thought we got lucky when we were assigned to this morning duty. All we had to do was stand outside and make sure the kids made it fifteen feet from the bus door to the front door of the community center. Seriously? Beats slinging hash in the breakfast line or organizing and supervising the kids' locker rooms.

Man, were we ever wrong. Corralling the kids from the bus to the front door is like herding kittens. Everyone wants to run in a different direction, like that ten seconds between stepping off the bus and being welcomed into the air-conditioned coolness of the community center is the only bit of freedom they will get all day. These kids are wild.

"Jack! This way, Jack. To the door. That's right." JC and I repeat the same lines over and over again as bus after bus arrives with more screaming campers.

I try to give high fives to all the kids as they exit the bus, which sometimes helps slow the mad dash to the door. I also try to say hi to every kid by name. If I don't know a name, I just call the kid "sport" or "champ" or "bud."

"Hi, Mr. Sam," they call, each one trying to slap my hand harder than the kid before them.

I spend the morning doing shooting, passing, and defense drills with small groups of kids. It's such a cushy job, playing basketball in an air-conditioned gym all summer, and I really like hanging out with the little kids. It makes me wonder what it would have been like to have brothers and sisters.

At lunch, JC and I grab a table in the middle of the giant multipurpose room, and bunches of kids join us. JC is one of the track-and-field coaches and one of the most popular with the kids. I tell him it's because of his winning personality. He says it's because all the kids want a chance to throw the javelin.

"They kiss my ass because they want to throw a spear like a gladiator or something. They're all kind of baffled when they come to track and field and I make them run the mile before I even show them the javelin," he says, laughing.

"You're such a hard-ass," I say.

"Attention, campers and staff!" We all turn toward the voice on the stage. Mr. Chapman is up there in a brand-new tracksuit, his whistle shiny around his neck. He's probably never even used it.

"Sadly, today is Mr. Tucker's last day. He is leaving us for a football position at the University of Rhode Island. Let's all give Mr. Tucker a round of applause!" We all clap while the campers hoot and whistle. One of the older campers brings a giant construction-paper card that all the kids have signed.

"Starting Monday, there will be a new face in our football program. Mr. Ace, will you come up here, please?"

"Oh, you've got to be kidding me," I say under my breath.

JC turns around and smirks at me. "See? A Broadmeadow football player."

I try to smile at JC. He loves it when his predictions are right.

Ace Quinn stands up from a table close to the front of the room while all the campers stand and clap for him. He waves to everyone, then catches sight of me not clapping. He touches two fingers to his right temple and then points them right at me in a mock salute.

I grit my teeth and salute back to him, but I know what he really meant: "I'm watching you."

The rest of the day is a complete bust. After lunch, I have three groups of older girls come through the basketball gym. All they want to do is talk about Ace.

"You go to school with him, right, Mr. Sam?"

"Doesn't he have the school record for most career passing yards and he's not even a senior yet?"

"I heard he's going to play football at the University of Texas after high school."

"I don't know about all that, but he sure is nice to look at."

Giggle, giggle, giggle.

"Just run, girls," I tell them.

They don't run, but at least they start moving toward the baseline.

"Football used to be my least favorite activity, but it just moved up a few notches on my list," one says to her friend.

"That's it. Suicides! Just run until I tell you to stop!" I say.

"Mr. Sam, you're no fun," one of them says, ruffling my hair on her way to the baseline.

I'm in a foul mood.

* * *

Grandpa is waiting for me when I get home from work.

"Ready, Sammy?" he says before I even have the front door completely open. "I've already got your gun in the case in the car. Let's get a move on!"

"Hey, Grandpa. My day was great, how was yours?" I mumble under my breath as I walk into the house. "Just let me put my stuff down," I say louder, motioning to the bag of basketball gear hanging from my shoulder.

"Don't be too long. Let's make hay while the sun shines, boy," he says as I head to my room.

Damn Grandpa and his damn guns. About a month after my dad died, Grandpa bought my mother a gun. "For self-defense," he told her.

Two weeks later, Grandpa and my mom got into this huge fight over it. Mom wanted to get rid of it. Grandpa wouldn't let her. "I'd never forgive myself if something happened to you or Sammy, Jenny. That's why I got it for you, honey. Please."

"I don't want this thing in my house! It scares me to death!" Mom went on a full rant then, saying she was worried that I would find it and shoot myself in the foot or something.

Grandpa countered by reminding her that Dean Quinn had been taking Ace out hunting and shooting since he was knee-high to a grasshopper.

I remember sitting in the kitchen, almost thirteen years old, watching them yell at each other and wondering if this was what my life was going to be like now. If this is what happens in houses where there isn't a father.

Finally, my mother relented after Grandpa promised to install a safe in the linen closet and store the bullets separately. Now once a month or so, Grandpa takes me to the shooting range to practice with the revolver. He loves it. I don't. I go because I have to. Because I know it keeps Mom from having to fight with him.

I change my shorts and throw a hat on my head before running back downstairs to meet Grandpa. I find him with my mom on the sunporch.

Mom is twisted into a pretzel shape, while Grandpa sits on a stool eating an apple.

"Hi, baby! How was work?" Mom says to me from the floor.

Shortly after Dad died, Mom stayed at a place called Morningside for awhile. At the time, Grandpa told me it was because she needed some peace and quiet. I knew it was a mental health treatment center, but we never talked about it. Just like with most things, Grandpa wasn't exactly open to a chat about his daughter's mental health status. It was there Mom first learned to do yoga, and now we find her tangled up on the sunporch more evenings than not.

"What is that?" I ask, gesturing toward her twisty limbs.

"One-Legged King Pigeon! Isn't it neat?" she asks, her legs all bent and one of her feet touching the back of her head. "You should try it with me. So relaxing."

"Yeah, sure." I smirk at Grandpa, and he gestures at me to shush. He's laughing behind his apple, though.

"We're headed out, Jenny. Don't get yourself all tangled up while we're gone." Grandpa kisses Mom on the head and winks at me.

When we're in the pickup, Grandpa turns the air conditioner on full blast. I turn it down a notch or two so I can talk to him.

"Did you know Ace got a job at the community center this summer? He starts on Monday," I say, trying to keep my voice steady.

"Is that right?" Grandpa says, smiling. "Well, good. A job would be good for him."

"What do you mean?" I ask.

"Oh, you know, Sammy." Grandpa squirms uncomfortably in his seat.

"No, I don't. What do you mean?"

Grandpa takes a deep breath, sucks his teeth and shakes his head a little bit. "You know, Ace is one of those kids. He's not like you, Sammy."

I raise my eyebrows. "How so?"

"You ever take a look at those trophies outside the gym at school?"

"Yeah," I say, shrugging. A special Student Athlete of the Year certificate with my name on it now sits in that trophy case, next to the certificates of other Broadmeadow athletes that won in previous years. It's the only proof I have that I even won that award since Ace smashed my trophy.

"Take notice of the names on most of those trophies?"

"Dean Quinn? Ace's dad?" I say, shrugging again. I don't see how Ace's dad winning trophies a million years ago has anything to do with Ace having a job.

"Ace needs something that's just his. Something he can excel at all on his own," Grandpa says, flicking the air conditioner back to full blast. That's Grandpa-ese for "This conversation is over."

It's an excuse I've heard a lot from Grandpa. Mr. Quinn expects a lot out of Ace. He rides him pretty hard. I couldn't feel bad for him. Who cares? So his dad is tough. Big deal. I think I was hoping that maybe Grandpa saw the change. Saw that Ace wasn't just a kid with a pushy dad anymore. Something was different.

* * *

I stare down the barrel of the .38 special and line up my sights. I only practice with the red bull's-eye targets. I can't bring myself to shoot at the people-shaped ones. The gun isn't heavy.

It isn't cold. The rubber grip fits right in my palm, my pointer finger curled around the trigger.

Grandpa is next to me in big, green earmuffs, watching how I line up my shot. He's making a face.

I lower the gun onto the counter in front of me and remove my own green earmuffs. Grandpa does the same. "Why are you making that face at me?" I ask him.

"You're lining it up all wrong. Plus it takes you too long. How many times do I have to tell you? If you've got a perp coming at you, you've only got a split second to raise the gun and shoot. You don't have time to stare down the barrel and line up a good shot. You've got to raise that gun and be ready to go. Now try it again."

I try not to roll my eyes at Grandpa. Instead, I wait until he gets his earmuffs back on, and I exhale really loudly through gritted teeth. We live in the suburbs. Yeah, I know, weird stuff happens every day, but it's almost like Grandpa expects something horrible to happen at any minute. *A perp. Jeez, Grandpa.* Sometimes I think he wishes he were a cop or something instead of a high-school football coach. He watches too much *CSI. Perp. For crying out loud.*

I lower the gun and put it on the counter in front of me. I try to pick it up quickly and shoot at the bull's-eye. I'm way off target, and I don't have time to prepare for the kick of the gun. My hand flies up and away from where it should be.

Grandpa shakes his head and removes his earmuffs. "You

need to be able to take only one shot, Sammy. It has to be done in one shot. Let's get out of here." He halfheartedly pats me on the back.

I open the cylinder and empty out the casings. The brass ends clink into the coffee can Grandpa brings to collect the shells.

Back in the car, Grandpa turns the air conditioner down two notches. He's biting the inside of his cheek and fidgeting back and forth in his seat.

"Something you want to talk about, Grandpa?" I ask, reading his cues.

"Yeah, there is, Sammy. Listen, your mother and I have been talking..."

Nothing good ever comes after those seven words.

"We think it might be time for me to sell my house. Your mom says there's room for me at the house with the two of you. I think I'm going to take her up on her offer."

"When is this going to happen?" I ask.

"Probably before the end of the summer. I told your mother I would talk to you about it. You gonna be okay with this, Sammy?" he says, not taking his eyes off the road even though we are stopped at a light.

"Yeah, I think it's a great idea," I say, even though I wonder if that's true or not.

"Your mom isn't really...Well, my house is just too much for me to take care of alone since your Grandma Mae died. It just doesn't make good sense. I think it will be good, Sammy," he says.

"What were you going to say about Mom? She isn't really what?" I know that Grandma Mae line is a load of bull. She's been gone for almost twenty years.

Grandpa just shakes his head. "Not important," he says.

I sigh, but not loudly enough for Grandpa to hear. *Mom isn't really what? Stable? No kidding. Happy? Well, duh. Able to take care of herself? That's why I'm there.*

"So what do you think? You'll take the upstairs bedroom, and I'll move into your old room?" he asks.

I nod.

"It's settled, then. We'll tell your mom when we get back home." Gramps turns the AC up three notches. He's done talking.

5

JULY
Ten Months Before

My mom and I only missed the Sandy Grove Neighborhood Fourth of July party once since we moved here. The year my dad died, I couldn't get Mom out of the house. I decided to go by myself, but only got to the end of my street before I gave up and went back home. All of those kids with their dads...I couldn't do it. I went home and sat on the couch with Mom. We watched the fireworks from our living-room window that night and didn't speak.

This year, I can only think of Marnie. The year after I spent the night on the couch with Mom, Marnie insisted that I come to the party with her family, even if my mom didn't want to go. I still remember she was wearing Statue of Liberty sunglasses and knocked on my door with a pair for me.

"Ready?" she asked, grabbing my hand and putting the sunglasses on my face. She pulled me out the door, not giving me a chance to say no.

Later that afternoon, Mom found her way to the party too. The Keatons invited her to sit with them for the barbecue. The Quinns joined us later on, and even Ace was kind of nice to me that year. Marnie held my hand during the fireworks. We were thirteen.

"I've got the dandelion greens. Can you carry the Jell-O salad, Sam? I've got my hands full," Mom calls from the kitchen.

"I'm putting everything in the wagon, Mom. We can put the greens and the Jell-O in there too. I've already got the cooler and the chairs loaded up." I'm trying to hurry Mom along. All I can think about is Marnie. It's the day of my self-imposed deadline, and I'm determined not to chicken out.

Grandpa comes through the front door with an armload of cardboard boxes. "All ready for the barbecue?"

"I wish you'd come with us, Dad. You know everyone would love to see you," my mom says.

"Oh, you go ahead and have fun. You don't need an old man around tonight," he says, patting her back. "I've got plenty of boxes to unload, anyway. I'll be busy all night."

His eyes are shiny, and I know he's been sitting on the porch drinking beer. The Fourth of July does it for him every year. My grandmother passed away on the Fourth almost twenty years ago. Grandpa doesn't do the Fourth.

"I know it's not easy, Dad, but you really—"

"That's enough, Jenny," Grandpa says, his eyebrows raised. His voice is stern. It's his football coach voice. We don't hear it often around the house.

I watch the two of them stare at each other and get an uneasy feeling in my stomach. I can hear the second hand on the kitchen clock ticking. Neither one of them wants to be the one to look away first. My mother has her defiant face on, chin jutted out and nose in the air.

"Jenny, I'm sorry," Grandpa says.

Mom stares at him for one more beat before turning her back.

"Let's not forget the zucchini bread, Sam. You know how much Mrs. Macmillan loves my zucchini bread. Did you pack my sparkling water? You know I can't sit in the heat without it."

She plops her floppy straw hat on her head and tosses a brown prescription bottle into her shoulder bag. She paints sunscreen on her nose until it almost glows.

Grandpa puts down the boxes, grabs a beer from the refrigerator, and retreats to the screen porch.

"You know he doesn't do the Fourth," I whisper to my mom.

"I just thought if we could get him out of the house..." Mom takes a deep breath through her nose. "It's hard for all of us," she says, digging through her bag for the pill bottle she just threw in there.

"I know, but Grandpa—"

"We don't have to talk about it anymore," Mom says, popping a tiny white pill into her mouth and tossing the bottle back into her bag.

I grit my teeth. We don't have to talk about it. It's not the right time now.

I think I'll ask Mrs. Macmillan to crochet that on a pillow for us.

"The water is in the cooler. You ready?"

Mom nods and we head out the door, dragging the wagon full of dandelion greens and Jell-O salad and sparkling water behind us. My phone buzzes in my front pocket. I pull it out and see a text from Marnie.

We're here! Are you?

My cheeks burn and I feel a smile pulling on my lips. I text back: Walking now. Be right there ☺

The party is in full swing when we reach the end of the main road. The neighborhood's private beach is buzzing with people. Kids are chasing each other in the sand with sparklers, and some of the moms are gossiping with their toes in the surf. Someone has set up a game of horseshoes, and a group of people is gathered around that.

I park the wagon in a shady spot for Mom and look around the beach for Marnie. Not too many years ago, I was chasing her with a sparkler while my mom gossiped with her toes in the water and my dad dominated the horseshoe pit.

Staring out at the water, I feel someone jump on my back and wrap her arms around my neck. "You're here!" Marnie yells in my ear. "No Grandpa?" she whispers.

I just shake my head.

"I'm sorry," she whispers, her breath tickling my ear.

JC saunters down the beach toward Marnie and me.

"Finally made it?" he asks.

"Mom needed to get her Jell-O salad ready," I say, shrugging as Marnie hops down.

"Looks like Mrs. Macmillan is already lit," JC says, pointing to the horseshoe game. She laughs loudly and swings a horseshoe way over her head. It lands with a splash right by the gossiping moms.

"Same shit, different year," I say, laughing.

I watch my mom walk around the periphery of the party. She looks uncomfortable. And sad. I have to look away.

Marnie, JC, and I walk down the beach and find a spot to sit away from the screaming, sparkler-wielding kids. "Remember when we all used to do that?" Marnie asks, bumping up against my shoulder.

My face burns when I look at her and nod. "Doesn't seem that long ago."

"It wasn't that long ago, you dorks. We were screwing around like that last year!" JC says, hurling a rock into the ocean.

"Look, Ace is here!" Marnie stands up and points down the beach.

Sure enough, Ace is sauntering toward us through the sand, shirtless and shoeless. Marnie takes off running to meet him.

"Great, Mr. Wonderful has arrived," I say.

"Just chill, Sam. Let it go," JC says quietly.

"Tonight I was gonna…Marnie. You know," I say.

"And now you can't?" JC asks, eyebrows raised.

"He just complicates everything."

"Only because you let him."

"He's constantly right there. Right in my face," I say.

"Wait a minute, wait a minute…I thought all that business with him stopped after…when we were twelve?" JC says.

"After my dad died? It's okay. You can say it."

"Yeah. After that. I thought he stopped."

I didn't tell him, or anyone, what really happened to my trophy at the Student Athlete Awards. About Ace breathing like a bull and looking ready to take my head off. The look in his eyes. It's true; I had almost five years of relative peace before this new, more sinister Ace showed up at the awards ceremony. Relative peace. I mean, he was still the same pigheaded blowhard, but at least I wasn't directly in the line of fire. But now? Something has shifted.

"Seriously, Sam. We're about to be seniors. You've got to let that shit go," he says.

You didn't see him that night in the bathroom after the awards. If you had, you wouldn't be telling me to let shit go.

"What's up, girls!" Ace says as he and Marnie approach JC and me.

"Hey, Ace," JC says, holding his hand up for a high five.

I ignore him and look instead at Marnie. Her arm is around Ace's bicep, and she's staring up at him with big, moony eyes. She's been staring at him like that since we were little kids. My gut falls to my knees. There goes my plan.

"How are you liking the community center, Ace?" JC says.

"Can't complain. It would be nice to have a few more hotties to look at, though. Why don't you get a job there, Keaton? Give me something to look at," he says, grabbing Marnie around the waist and tickling her ribs.

Marnie giggles and tries to twist away from the tickling. Her rear end bumps Ace's thigh, and he gives her a hearty smack right on the butt. The heat rises up my chest.

"Some of those camper groups are pretty hot, though. That seventh-grade girl group? Am I right, Cushman?" Ace laughs, his mouth gaping open so wide I can see the back of his throat. I'd like to stick my fist in there.

Marnie backs up from Ace. "Did you seriously just say that?" She laughs and covers her mouth.

"Yeah, so? It's true! Even Sammy thinks so. Don't you, Sammy?" Ace nudges me hard in the ribs.

"No," I say into the sand. My face turns red. Marnie is

staring at me.

"See! Sammy's turning red! He's been checking out the little girls!" Ace puts his hand on Marnie's hip and squeezes. She snorts.

"I think I'm going swimming," I say, walking toward the bathhouse.

"Wait up," Marnie calls, jogging in the sand away from Ace and JC. My face burns. I clutch my fists at my sides. "Don't worry about Ace. He's just kidding. He's just a kidder like that," she says.

"Yeah, he's a kidder. Those girls he's talking about are only like twelve, Marn."

"Well, he's just joking. He's not going to seriously hit on a seventh grader, for crying out loud. I know Ace's sense of humor."

We stay quiet all the way to the bathhouse. I want to say more, but something heavy hangs between Marnie and me. She doesn't reach for my bicep and hang on like she did to Ace just a little while ago. I don't want this to bother me.

I walk into the water and dive under, resurfacing and turning around just in time to see Marnie coming out of the bathhouse. She's wearing a one-piece bathing suit with a towel wrapped around her waist. She looks beautiful. I stick my head under the water again.

She swims underwater until she reaches me. Her eyelashes drip when she comes up for air just inches from my face. We tread water and look at each other. I want to put my hands on her like Ace did a little while ago. I want to know what her skin feels like under my palm.

"Race you to the buoy," she says, putting her hand on my head and pushing me under as she starts kicking toward the orange buoy about fifty feet away.

"Cheater!" I yell, kicking and swimming as fast as I can to catch up with her.

"The crowd goes wild! Keaton wins the gold! Keaton wins the gold!" Marnie reaches the buoy first and pumps her fist above her head.

I halfheartedly paddle my way out to her, a full five seconds behind. "Cheaters never win, Keaton!" I laugh.

"You're no fun," she says, laughing and touching her finger to my nose. I grab on to the buoy with her, and we bob in the waves together. Our feet touch underwater.

The salt water clings to her skin, and her eyes are shining in the sunlight. Our feet touch again.

So I kiss her.

And she kisses me back.

"Race you back to shore," she says, pulling out of the kiss.

"Wait. Maybe I wasn't done yet," I say, reaching for her waist underwater.

"*If* you win this time, maybe I'll let you do it again," Marnie says, pushing off of the buoy and out of my reach.

I dive under and kick as hard as I can, the feel of her salty lips on mine driving me forward faster than I thought I could go.

I reach the shore just one arm length ahead of Marnie. "I'm the winner!" I say, completely out of breath. I collapse in the sand as Marnie crawls up.

"Maybe I let you win that time," she says, sitting in the sand next to me, her thigh touching mine.

"Oh yeah? Why's that?" I ask.

"Maybe I wanted the prize too," she says, leaning in and biting her bottom lip.

I bend down and kiss her again. Slower this time.

"Hot damn! Leave you two alone for five minutes, and already you're rolling around in the sand!" Ace yells from down the beach. Three or four freshman girls are with him, and they all giggle at his stupid joke.

Marnie laughs too. "Shut up, Ace," she says, standing up and brushing the sand from her suit.

She walks back down the beach toward the barbecue, winking back at me over her shoulder. The freshman girls follow behind her like a flock of baby geese, leaving Ace and me alone.

"What are you even doing, Samantha?" he says in a soft voice.

"What are you talking about?"

"With Marnie? You like her? You want to bone her? You're a loser. She's not going to sleep with you. You'd be better off trying to sink your pecker into your buddy JC. He'd probably take it up the ass from you."

"Shut the hell up, Ace," I say. I try to stand up as straight as I can, but I'm still an inch or so shorter than him. I know he can see my heart pounding against my ribs from where he's standing.

You're not twelve years old anymore, Sam. You're bigger, stronger, smarter—

"Seriously, I'm just trying to help you out. You have no chance, dickweed. No chance. I just want to save you any humiliation. You'll see," he says, shaking his head and smirking.

I keep my distance from Ace for the rest of the night. If he comes near, I make sure I move away. I can feel him watching me, though. I can feel it right through my skin.

When the sun finally falls below the horizon, JC's dad hauls out the fireworks. He and JC busy themselves at the end of the dock, setting up complicated-looking wooden rigs. I watch my mom try to have a conversation with Mrs. Macmillan. I can almost hear my mom trying to tell Mrs. Macmillan the finer points of her zucchini bread recipe. I hope Mrs. Macmillan is at least pretending to listen.

I look for Marnie and find her with the little kids, helping to light sparklers and hand them out. "Want to watch with me?" I ask her.

"Of course." She smiles and bites her bottom lip again.

I motion down the beach with my chin, and she nods. I

shove my hands in my pockets, and Marnie holds on to my bicep. My cheeks burn.

We find a quiet spot in the sand close to where we were before and sit down. We both stare out at the ocean and the sinking sun.

We look out at the horizon for a long time without speaking. It's comfortable, though. Easy. Marnie doesn't move her hand from my arm.

I lean in and kiss her again. I touch her cheek, and she puts her hand on my knee. I can see the red and blue glow of the fireworks even with my eyes closed. I put my hand on her leg, and she doesn't move or flinch. My hand traces the smooth line from her thigh to her hip to her waist. I pull her closer to me, and she puts her hand on my hip and squeezes.

I stop kissing her, and she rests her forehead on mine.

"Does this mean...I mean, are we..." I can't bring myself to say the words. My eye twitches, and my heart pounds in my throat.

"Do you think we need to define this like that? Can't we just be...what we are?" she asks, her voice barely above a whisper.

I don't even know what that means. I kiss her again. Hard. Her breath catches in her throat, and a tiny noise escapes. My insides are on fire.

"We can be what we are. What are we?" I say, my lips on her neck now.

She giggles and puts her hand on my chest. "We escape

definition," she says, suddenly standing up and pulling on my hands. "Come on, let's take a walk on the pier." She laughs, her face bright and lips swollen.

I watch her from my spot in the sand for a minute. Her green eyes dance in the glow of the fireworks in front of us. "Sure. Just let me change out of this bathing suit, okay? Wait for me outside the bathhouse?"

Marnie nods. She bends at her waist for another kiss. A short one this time.

I grab my bag and head toward the men's changing room. The light is yellow and dim, and the mirrors are foggy from the salt water. The floor is covered with grime and sand, and my toes curl. I know I should have worn my flip-flops in here. Gross.

I throw my wet suit in the bag and try to wash some of the salt from the mirror with my damp towel. I lean over the sink and get as close to the mirror as I can.

"Samantha," I hear spoken quietly behind me.

My chest tightens and I turn around.

"What the fuck, Ace," I say.

He is just inches from me. I didn't even hear him come into the bathhouse. My toes dig into the grimy floor. Ace's breathing is shallow like it was the night of the awards.

"What do you think you're doing?" he says quietly, a sneer forming on his lips.

I can feel his breath on my face and the heat radiating from his bare chest.

"She's not going to stay with you, Samantha. She's a little slut, and she's always looking for the next best thing. Why don't you just give up your little fantasy?" he says, shuffling his feet even closer to me.

The cold stainless-steel sink digs into my lower back as Ace gets closer and closer to my face. My heart is pounding so hard I know he can hear it. This isn't the harmless all-talk Ace I've come to avoid and ignore for the past five years. This Ace is different. I feel like a gazelle trapped in a lion's cage.

"Not to mention," he says, "that you're dickless. Little Marnie Slutbag doesn't want a dickless boyfriend," he says, grabbing the waistband of my shorts and pulling. My feet slip on the grimy floor, and I tighten my grip on the edge of the sink.

"Watch out, Samantha. Watch. Out," he says, poking a finger into my sternum.

He turns and walks out of the bathhouse. My feet are glued to the nasty floor, and I finally exhale in a loud puff. I turn around at the sink and splash cold water on my face and try to catch my breath. I will my heart to stop racing. I know Marnie is out there waiting for me. She can't see me like this. I squeeze my eyes shut and try to remember some of Mom's yoga breathing techniques. Three long, deep breaths from the bottoms of your feet.

Outside the bathhouse, Marnie is waiting for me. And talking to Ace.

"You guys taking a walk to the pier?" he asks with a smile when he sees me.

"Yeah, you want to come with us?" Marnie answers him with a smile as big as the sun.

Oh god no. No. No, no, no.

He looks at me and smirks. "No, that's okay. You guys have fun."

I grab Marnie's hand and stand up as straight as I can. We turn and walk toward the pier. I look back over my shoulder at Ace, standing shirtless in the pool of yellow light outside the bathhouse.

"Watch it," he mouths, crossing his arms over his chest.

6

AUGUST
Nine Months Before

"Two-a-days suck," JC says to me as he gets into my truck, throwing his football pads into the bed.

"Good morning to you too, sunshine," I say, laughing.

"Can't you convince Grandpa that we're good enough without the two-a-days in the middle of August?"

"Do you think we are?"

"Hell, no," JC says, closing his eyes and leaning his head on the window.

"Well, there you go, then," I say, readjusting the AC vent to blow right on my forehead.

Grandpa gets to football practice way before JC and I do. He and Ace are already looking over the playbook when we arrive. Ace's dad stands at the fence nearby as usual, his Broadmeadow cap perched on his head. Since Ace made the varsity team his freshman year, Mr. Quinn has been a permanent fixture on the sidelines at football practice. He's just part of the scenery now, like the scoreboard or sponsor signs hanging in the end zone. It would be weird if he wasn't there.

"Hey, QB2! Get enough beauty sleep?" Ace yells to me when he sees me coming.

Both Grandpa and Mr. Quinn laugh. They think it's just good-natured razzing, but I know better. I can't think of a snappy retort, so I just keep my mouth shut. JC trudges off to the far side of the field with the other running backs while I approach Ace and Grandpa.

"Coach Franklin," I say when I get there, nodding my head at Grandpa. On the field, he insists that I call him Coach Franklin. I get it.

"I was just showing Ace the playbook for the season, Sammy. I'm going to leave you guys to it for a bit and address the other players. Field house in thirty. Okay, boys?" he says, jogging away and not waiting for an answer.

"Coach! Can I get your ear for a second?" Mr. Quinn yells to Grandpa, jogging down the fence line toward the visiting end zone.

I'm stuck standing alone with Ace on the sidelines. I grit my teeth because I don't want to ask him to show me the plays. But I also know I'll be in deep shit if I don't at least know what

Grandpa is referring to when we have our team meeting in the field house in thirty minutes.

"How much is this worth to you?" Ace asks, holding up the playbook and throwing a quick glance downfield to where his dad has caught up with Grandpa.

I shrug like it doesn't matter, but Ace knows better.

"Oh, QB2, quit fucking with me," Ace says with a smile.

"Quit screwing around. I don't want to be here either. Let's just get the plays down and get it over with," I say.

Surprisingly, Ace just smirks and sits on the bench, opening the book. We look at plays together for a solid ten minutes without talking.

"So...tell me about Ms. Marnie Slutbag," Ace says.

Immediately I get defensive. "What about her? And don't call her that."

"Relax, QB2. I just mean you're together, right?"

I exhale. "Yeah."

Ace shakes his head and lets out a guffaw.

I want to ignore it. Really, I do. The truth is, I don't know what Marnie and I are doing. Are we together? I say yes. We haven't talked about it since the Fourth of July. She comes over a lot. And we spend a lot of time together in my room. Or at the lifeguard stand at the beach. So are we together? Yeah. Unless we're not.

Last night, I heard a quiet *plink, plink, plink* on my window. I opened the shades, and there she was in my driveway with a handful of pebbles. Three a.m. I threw on a T-shirt and ran outside.

"Why didn't you just call me?" I said.

"I kind of like being retro...throwing rocks at your window," she answered, wrapping her arms around my waist and kissing me hard.

"Everything okay?" I asked, kissing her back.

"Meh," she said. "Just don't want to be alone."

We started walking, heading toward the beach.

"Remember when we were on a basketball team together in kindergarten?" I asked her.

"Of course I remember that! The Bumblebees! We had yellow and black jerseys, and your dad was the coach." Marnie laughed. "I remember he spent the entire season making sure every kid on the team got to score at least once. The last game of the season, I was the only kid who hadn't scored. He told everyone on the team to give me the ball every single time we went down the court. I finally scored one basket in the final seconds of the game." She laughed again.

"I remember that too. The Bumblebees...Feels like a million years ago," I say, smiling at the memory of my dad and kindergarten Marnie.

"I remember that when I scored that basket, your dad came out onto the court and lifted me up in the air. He ran up and down the court with me like that while everyone cheered," she said, laughing. "That was the beginning and the end of my basketball career!"

We reached the lifeguard stand and climbed up.

"I remember how sad it was when he died," Marnie said.

We settled into the lifeguard chair, our thighs touching. "I remember you were the only one who didn't ignore me right after it happened," I said to her. I reached out and held her hand.

She shrugged next to me. "I was just doing what I thought would help," she said.

It meant a lot to me, I thought but didn't say. *More than you'll ever know.*

Marnie had come to my dad's wake with her parents. She'd pulled me aside and given me a hug.

"I'm sorry," she said. "This blows some serious chunks."

It wasn't eloquent. It wasn't sensitive. But it was the most real thing anyone had said to me in days.

For the rest of the wake, Marnie sat in the back row of chairs. Her parents left, but Marnie asked to stay. Every so often, I'd look back and she'd smile. "You okay?" she'd mouth. "No," I'd mouth back. She formed a heart with her hands and held it close to her chest every time I glanced her way.

When I went back to school a week or so later, there was Marnie. She didn't avoid me like most of the other kids did, and she never said the things the adults said to me in those first few days. "Your memories of him will help you through this." Or "Be strong. That's what he would have wanted." Never

ever "He's in a better place." As well meaning as some of those things are, they're not helpful.

"I brought you an extra PB and J" is what Marnie said at lunch that day. She reached into her lunch bag and handed me a sandwich. Then she pointed to a table full of cheerleaders in the center of the cafeteria. "There's an empty seat on the end. You wouldn't have to talk to anyone but me if you didn't want to."

I sat with her for two weeks. Some days we talked. Some days I talked to the other girls at the table. Mostly, though, I just sat and didn't talk to anyone.

When everyone started to forget that I was "that kid whose father died," I slowly started eating lunch at my old table. Marnie didn't ask any questions. She'd walk by me every day, though, and drop a sandwich or a pack of peanut-butter crackers on my tray.

She was always close.

Ace lets out a loud sigh and chuckles next to me. I was so lost in my thoughts about Marnie that I almost forgot where I was.

"What was that for?" I say, gritting my teeth.

"Nothing, QB2. Nothing at all," he says, laughing again.

We look back down at the playbook, jotting notes in the margins.

"Have you been with her yet?" Ace asks nonchalantly.

"What do you mean? Have I slept with her? That's none of

your business," I say, biting the inside of my cheek so hard that I taste blood.

"Oh come on, Samantha. Give it up. What's she like? Loose or tight? Maybe I'll take a piece of that when you're done with it," he says.

That's it. That's all I can take. I stand up and shove Ace's shoulder as hard as I can. Fire burns in my chest hotter than the fear this time. "You'd better shut up," I say.

"Or what? You'll kick my ass?" Ace laughs, but he's not smiling. He stands up and gives my shoulder a small but solid push.

I'm caught off balance and I fall into the grass. I turn and see Grandpa coming toward us. Ace sees him too, and reaches his hand down to help me up. "Sorry about that, Sam. I didn't mean to knock you down," he says a little too loudly. He pulls me to my feet with a big, greasy smile on his face.

"Everything okay over here?" Grandpa asks as he approaches.

"Yes, sir. Just horsing around," Ace says.

Grandpa looks at me. I nod and look at the ground.

"You know better than that, Quinn. Give me five laps around the field. Full pads and helmet. And you better not be late to the field house."

Ace stares at Grandpa.

"Go on," Grandpa says. "You heard me."

"Why doesn't he have to run? He pushed me first," Ace says.

Grandpa's face turns stormy. "You're gonna question me, boy?"

"No, sir," Ace says, pulling his helmet over his head.

"I didn't think so," Grandpa says, glaring at Ace. "Carry these playbooks to the field house, North," he says to me, handing me a stack of binders and walking away.

Ace glares at me when Grandpa leaves.

"Unbelievable. If we go to state this year, you need to remember that QB2 doesn't play at state. And he doesn't get the girl either. I told you to fucking watch yourself, Sam. I mean it," Ace says when Grandpa is out of earshot.

* * *

Marnie calls when I'm on my way home from practice.

"What's going on with you tonight?" she says.

"I'm up for anything. What did you have in mind?"

"There's a party on East Beach. Kind of an end-of-summer thing. Should we go?"

"Of course we should. Do you want to come over here and we'll walk down? Around seven or so?" I ask.

"I'll be there. And Sam?"

"Yeah?"

"My life would suck without you." She giggles.

"You're gonna miss me when I'm gone," I answer.

"You're the wind beneath my wings!"

"Umm...You ain't nothing but a hound dog?" I laugh.

"Oh god. You should be disqualified for that one," Marnie

says, laughing.

"I'll see you in a few hours," I say.

"Can't wait," she replies quietly. I can hear her smile through the phone.

I hang up and pull my pickup into the driveway. Mom's old Volkswagen is already there, even though she's supposed to be at work. I can see from where I'm parked that the living room blinds are still closed.

"Mom?" I call when I unlock the front door.

"In here," she answers from the back of the house.

She is wrapped in my dad's old bathrobe and is sitting under her desk on the sunporch. I sit down on the floor next to the desk.

"How long?" I ask.

This isn't the first time I've found Mom under her desk, wrapped up in my dad's old clothes. She says that every once in a while, the sadness overwhelms her and she feels like she can't move. I judge whether I have to call her therapist on how long she's been under there. An hour or so? Not so bad. All day? I'm glad I have the therapist saved in my contacts.

"Just an hour. I'll be okay, Sammy. How was practice?" she asks.

"Do you want me to call Cathy?" The therapist.

"I'll be okay," she says.

"But you didn't go to work."

m fine," she says, an edge creeping into her voice.

having a bonfire. It's not that important, Mom. I can stay home," I say.

"Oh, don't be silly. I'm fine. Today was hard, but not something I can't get through on my own. You go get JC," she says, standing up. She wipes the grass from her legs and takes off my dad's robe. "Can you hang this up on the back of my door on your way out?"

I take it from her and meet her eyes. "You sure?"

She nods and swallows hard. I see her mouth turn down a little bit, but she puts her head down and walks back into the house. I pull out my phone and make sure I still have Therapist Cathy in my contacts.

I pull my truck into JC's driveway and beep the horn. His mom comes out onto the porch and waves me in with a great, big smile. I smile back at her because I can't help it. I turn off the engine and get out of the cab.

"Hi, honey bun! How's my Sam?" JC's mom pulls me into a hug. She used to play college basketball a million years ago, and she's well over six feet tall. When I was little, I was afraid I was going to be swallowed whole when she hugged me. I'm a little braver now, but it's still sometimes shocking to be hugged by a woman who towers over me.

"Hi, Mrs. Cushman. I'm doing good," I say.

"And your mom? How is she holding up?"

I try not to think of Mom squeezed under the desk in Dad's blue bathrobe. "She's okay," I lie.

"Well, come inside. Jay Jay will be ready in a minute." She tucks me under her arm and pulls me inside.

JC's dad is a good foot shorter than his mom. An engineering professor–mad scientist, he always has fourteen different projects in fourteen different stages of completion on the dining-room table. The Cushmans never eat in the dining room. They only eat on TV trays in the living room. Even if JC brings a girl over for dinner, they eat on the trays.

"Whatcha working on, Mr. C?" I ask JC's dad, who is bent over the dining-room table with a complicated harness on his head that holds a tiny penlight and a magnifying glass over his right eye.

"Oh, you know...just tinkering..." he answers. I try to make sense of the wires and tiny screws and circuit boards on the table so I can ask another question. But looking at it just makes me dizzy. I watch in silence for a few more seconds before JC comes down the stairs.

"Ready, bro?" he asks, reaching for his coat.

"Let's motor," I tell him.

A quick hug for Mrs. Cushman, and we are on our way.

"Has Jeannie been calling you or something?" I ask him in the safety of the truck.

He shrugs. "Maybe."

"Quit messing around. Has she or hasn't she?"

"She texted me this morning and asked if I would be there. I don't know where she got my number," he says.

"Maybe Marnie."

"I don't even care. I mean, did you see her at the last bonfire? All that dark hair. Those librarian glasses. And she was wearing these boots, Sam. The boots," he says, laying his head back with a groan.

"Were they, like, magic boots or something?" I laugh.

"Shut up, turd burglar," JC says, but he's smiling.

We pull back into my driveway just as Marnie comes up the front walk.

"Bae!" she calls and waves.

I smile.

JC makes puking noises next to me.

"Jealous," I say.

"After tonight, Jeannie Kruger is going to be calling me all kinds of gushy names. Just wait."

"Hey, just let me check on my mom real quick, and then I'll be ready to go," I tell JC and Marnie.

"Oh, let me come in and say hi!" Marnie says.

"Nah, Mom's not feeling good," I tell her. "She's a little under the weather. I wouldn't want you to catch anything."

Marnie accepts my excuse, and I head inside. Mom is sitting on the couch now with a knitting project in her lap. There is no sign of the blue bathrobe. "I'm headed out now," I tell her.

"You be safe, Sam. Curfew at one," she says.

"You sure you're okay? I can stay home, you know. We can watch a movie. *The Music Man*? Your favorite," I say.

"Sam! I'm fine. I promise. Go have fun." she says.

Grandpa comes out of the kitchen and nods at me.

"When did you get home?" I ask.

"Just a little bit ago," he says, drying a water glass with a dish towel. Then he mouths where Mom can't see, "I'm here. It's okay."

I give Grandpa a small smile and nod and kiss Mom on the top of her head. I notice she has Cathy's business card in her hand. "Do you want me to call Cathy before I go?" I ask, pointing to the card.

"This?" She holds up the card. "I've already called her. Now get." She shoos me out the door.

Mom's saying all the right things, but there's a heaviness in her voice that I haven't heard since my dad died.

"Mom okay?" Marnie asks when I get back to the car.

Is Mom okay?

Not really?

I don't think so?

Definitely not?

Marnie stares at me with wide eyes, waiting for an answer. She puts her hand on my knee.

"I...Yeah. She's okay," I say with a really fake smile. "She's okay."

7

TODAY
4:48 p.m.

"How long have you known Marnie Keaton?"

I don't answer.

"A long time, right? You two went to elementary school together, didn't you?"

I don't answer.

"Live in the same neighborhood. Is that right?"

I don't answer.

Michael sighs, rubbing his eyes. A loud, long exasperated sigh.

"Look at me, Sam," he says, unbuttoning his sleeves and methodically rolling them up his hairy arms.

I raise my eyes to meet his. My mouth stays firmly closed.

"I'm here to help you. I will get you out of this room and to your mom as quickly as I can, but you have to help me out. Do you understand that?"

Mom.

I nod.

"Okay, good. Let's talk about Ms. Keaton," he says, his pen poised over the folder.

Ms. Keaton. Marnie. With her brown hair and her loud, snorty laugh.

Marnie, kissing my face and squeezing my hand.

Marnie, touching my knee and smiling her special Sam smile, her bottom lip tucked between her teeth.

Marnie, putting her hand up.

Telling me not to.

Yelling "don't!".

"No," I say.

"No?"

"Not Marnie."

Michael stares at me for a full minute. I stare right back. He works his tongue over his front teeth, clicking the end of his pen several times.

"If I talk about something other than Marnie, will you answer my questions?" he asks.

I nod twice.

"Tell me about your dad."

My stomach drops. Another quake of pain rattles my forehead, my cheeks, my throat. It settles in my ribs.

"How long has he been gone?" Michael asks, his voice softer now.

"Five years," I say.

I feel the familiar twist in my chest while I count the years in my head.

"You were pretty young when he died," Michael says.

"Middle school," I say.

"That must have been difficult."

My heart speeds up. "That's not why this happened. Me and my mom...we're okay. This has nothing to do with—"

"I didn't say it did, Sam," Michael puts his hand on mine and squeezes. "Take a breath."

I do.

"Would you feel better if we moved on to something else?"

I nod once.

"James Cushman," Michael says, adjusting his heavy frame in the creaky chair.

"JC?" I say, scratching at my wrist. The skin pulses underneath my fingertips.

"Is that what you call him? JC, then. Tell me about JC," he says.

I take a deep breath in through my nose and close my eyes.

"Can we talk about JC?" Michael says.

I open my eyes a little and turn my head away.

The window in the room looks out over the roof of the building. There's steam floating along the black tar.

Industrial-looking machines chug away out there, puffing smoke into the air. I watch the smoke curl and swirl and dance into the cloudless sky.

"Sam?" Michael says again, scooting his chair just a hair closer to me.

"JC's my best friend," I say, my voice unsteady.

"Is he?"

I jerk my head and look at Michael. "Yes."

My heart jumps into my throat. Where is JC? I frantically try to piece together a timeline of this afternoon. JC was there. The gun went off. Did I see him again after that?

"Is he okay? Where is he right now?" I try to keep my voice even, but it sounds weird coming out of my mouth.

"He's fine, Sam. I promise," Michael looks me right in the eye.

I search his face for any sign that he might be lying to me. He doesn't even blink. I believe him.

"Does JC know what's been going on with you the past few weeks?" Michael says, scratching something in his notebook.

"JC and I...we haven't exactly been close for...awhile," I say.

"Can you tell me more about that?"

No. No, I can't.

8

SEPTEMBER
Eight Months Before

JC and I are in charge of the ring-toss booth. The Football Carnival is the biggest event of the school year at Broadmeadow. The senior football players and cheerleaders are each charged with running a booth, while the underclassmen have to do the crappy jobs like serve popcorn and funnel cakes and clean up after the pony rides. For three days in mid-September, the football field is transformed into a blinking, glowing cacophony of carnival sights and smells. It brings in a load of cash for the football and cheerleading programs; I've heard Grandpa talking about it.

"Step right up and try your luck, folks! Five rings for a buck. What a steal! Look at these prizes...Step right up. Step right up!" Whoever decided to give JC a bullhorn should be strung up by his toenails.

"Sit down, would ya? I think you're scaring all the customers away," I say, pulling on his football jersey.

"Slow day," JC says, sitting down next to me and turning off the bullhorn.

"It'll pick up tonight. It always does," I say, juggling a few rings in the air.

"What booth is Marnie at?" JC asks.

"Face-painting," I say.

"What do you say? Should we go over and get Spider-Man makeovers like we used to when we were little? Might drum up a few visitors to the old ring-toss booth," he says, nudging me.

"You're a dork, JC."

He laughs and leaps over the edge of the booth. "I'm headed to get some lemonade from Jeannie…You want some?"

"I'm good," I say, stifling a yawn. I lean back in my chair and close my eyes behind my sunglasses.

"Hey, Mister Ring-Toss Man, can I get ten rings, please?" Marnie's voice wakes me up.

"Only ten? It might take you longer than that, miss," I say, getting out of my chair.

Marnie holds out two dollar bills and waits for her ten rings. I hold them just out of her reach. She pulls my jersey and gives me a long kiss on the lips, pulling the rings out of my hand at the same time.

"No one will win any stuffed animals for me, so I have to play all the games by myself," she says, faking a pout.

"What about your boyfriend?" I wink at her.

"Don't have one," she says, winking back and flipping her navy-blue cheerleader skirt up a little bit.

Marnie tosses her rings and doesn't come anywhere close to ringing a bottle. I hand her a tiny stuffed flamingo anyway.

"That's cheating," she says, holding the fuzzy pink bird to her cheek.

"Ten rings with no win is an automatic prize. I just made up that rule," I say. "Consider it a gift."

She leans over the edge of the booth and pulls on my jersey again. "I may have to think of a way to repay you for the gift," she says quietly, raising her eyebrows and kissing me again. "I think I'll name him Pinky Pete," she says, pushing my chest and walking away.

Her cheerleader skirt sways back and forth on her hips. She throws me a look over her shoulder, and all I can do is smile at her.

JC comes back about a half hour later, sweaty and holding two cups of lemonade. He flops down in the chair inside the booth.

"What took you so long?" I ask. "We had a hundred customers come through here while you were off doing who knows what."

"Did you really?"

"Jeez, you're gullible. Really, though, where've you been?"

JC says nothing, but downs both cups of lemonade and

then leans back in his chair. "I was a little busy," he says, smiling.

"Oh my god. Seriously? Again?"

JC just laughs.

"Is that all you guys do or what?"

"I don't kiss and tell," he says, the smile still on his face. "Come on, don't be such a prude. It's not like you and Marnie aren't—"

"We're not." I cut him off.

"Oh," JC says, his smile fading.

It's not that we don't want to. Well, it's not like I don't want to. Marnie's so hard to figure out. She's all over me one minute and then disappears for days at a time. I know it's because she's busy with cheerleading and our schedules don't always match up, but it's frustrating as hell. There are stretches of three, sometimes four, days in a row that I hear the pebbles on my window and we sneak out. It's always the same story: "I don't want to be alone," she'll say. One night last week we got caught in a rainstorm and had to run into the bathhouse until the lightning died down. We were so close that night. But after that, I didn't see her or even talk to her for five days.

Grandpa comes over to our booth around four. "Take an hour break, boys," he says. "It'll pick up tonight. Get yourself something to eat, and come back ready to work at five. Sound good?"

"Sounds good, Coach Franklin," JC says, saluting my grandfather.

JC and I lock up the money box and jump over the side of the booth. We wander over to the food booths and debate the merits of corn dogs versus giant turkey legs for dinner.

"Where are you applying for next year? Have you thought about it?" JC asks, settling down with his giant, drippy turkey leg.

"I've thought about it. My dad went to Oceanside...I think I'll apply there and maybe some other places."

The truth is that the only place I want to be is Oceanside. It's where my dad went. It's where he met my mom. Most of the stories I remember my dad telling revolved around the classes he took at Oceanside or the friends he met there. I think he'd be proud if I went there too. Like I'm following in his footsteps or something. I don't know. I can't explain all of that to JC without sounding like an assbucket, so I brush it off.

"Where are you applying?" I ask him. "As if I don't already know."

JC turns to look at me. "UConn," we say in unison.

"There's only one place for me," he says.

"Aren't you applying anywhere else, though? Closer to home?" I ask.

"Aww...are you going to miss me, shitmittens? I'll be home at Thanksgiving," JC says, whacking me in the forehead with his turkey leg.

"Oceanside has a decent basketball team," I say, wiping turkey juice from my brow with my T-shirt. "Maybe I can make it as a walk-on or something."

"A walk-on? Are you kidding me? Man, you're going to have scouts all over you this winter. Just wait. They'll be offering you scholarships left and right. I can't wait for basketball season," JC says.

"Yeah, why in the hell did we join the football team anyway? Neither of us ever gets to play," I say.

JC looks at me and shrugs. "Cheerleaders?"

I laugh. "Hey, let's get our home jerseys out of the truck for tonight before we forget. Grandpa wants us to wear them, remember?"

We head toward the student parking lot and notice a small crowd of football players and cheerleaders gathered around a black Jeep. I can hear Ace Quinn's big mouth all the way across the lot.

"...Dad said I could have any car on the lot. This one just called my name, though," he is saying, patting the hood of the Jeep. "We had the gun rack installed, and I picked it up this morning," he adds, running his hands over the two-gun harness attached to the roll bar near the backseat.

JC and I wander over to the crowd. "What's going on, party people?" JC asks, exchanging high fives with some of the other players.

"Quinn's dad got him a Jeep," one of the safeties says.

"As congratulations. I was offered a football scholarship," Ace says, pulling a rag from his back pocket and running it over that gun rack.

"Oh yeah? Cool. Where?" JC says.

"ECC," Ace says, jutting his chin out a little bit.

"Easthaven Community College?" I say, smiling.

Ace looks up at me. "Yeah. I'm not going there. But my dad was so excited about the scholarship that he bought me the Jeep. Wonder what he'll do when I get into Texas."

"Hook 'em Horns! Right, Ace?" one of the underclassmen yells, punching Ace in the bicep.

"Yeah. Hook 'em Horns," Ace says slowly, still staring at me.

I check my watch and see that we only have a few minutes to get back to our booths. I poke JC in the side and motion to the football field. We start walking back, and the rest of the team follows.

"Hey, North. Come back. I want to show you something," Ace says as the crowd disperses.

"I really gotta get back, Ace. We only have an hour," I say, backing up.

"It'll only take a minute. Come on," Ace says, a wide smile pulling on his cheeks.

"I don't have time right now," I say, still backing up.

He slams the door to his Jeep and takes three heavy steps until he's directly in front of me. I stop moving. "You can go back in a minute," he says, pinching the front of my football jersey. The smile has disappeared, and I can see his jaw tensing.

Ace heads back toward the Jeep. I can tell by the way he's strutting that he knows I'm going to follow him. I do, my insides buzzing.

"It's almost hunting season, Samantha," he says, running the rag over the gun harness again. "Next month. Ducks and deer. You hunt, North?"

"No," I say, swallowing hard.

"You know what's the hardest thing about hunting? Of course you don't because you don't hunt. What kind of pussy doesn't hunt?"

I don't answer him.

"The hardest thing about hunting is sneaking up on your prey. You've got to be real quiet, you know? Lull them into thinking you're not even watching...you're not even there. But if you play your cards right, if you know just when to make your move..." Ace pounds his right fist into his left palm. "Pow. They don't even know what hit 'em."

I stare at Ace. He stares at me. His top lip curls and his nostrils flare.

"We gotta get back. Coach Franklin—"

"You mean dear old Grampy? I'm pretty sure he'll wait for his star QB."

I want to turn and run back to JC. Away from this parking lot.

"You got a problem with ECC, Samantha?" he says.

"No, I—"

"That's what I thought. The next time you make me look like a fool in front of the team, you're going to be breathing through your asshole," he says, poking a finger into my chest.

"I didn't say anything," I say, trying to back up.

He pinches my jersey again. "I'm not going to warn you again. Watch yourself," he says. "You remember what I'm capable of?"

"But I didn't—"

"Do I have to spell it out for you? I thought you were supposed to be some kind of genius. You make me look stupid, I will fuck you up. You tried it once when we were twelve, and do you remember what happened to you then? Do you understand now, Samantha?"

"I didn't even say anything..." I begin.

"Sam! Your grandpa is looking for you." Marnie is jogging through the parking lot.

"Hey, Marnie!" Ace's smile returns, and he stops pulling on my jersey. "I was just showing Sam the new Jeep."

Marnie smiles and gives Ace a quick hug. "You going to bring me to school one day this week?"

"If it's okay with your boyfriend," Ace says. His eye twitches just slightly, but his smile doesn't waver.

"I don't have a boyfriend," Marnie says, reaching for my hand and giving it a squeeze.

Ace's eyes settle on me, and he raises an eyebrow.

"Then it's settled. I'll pick you up tomorrow morning," he says to her.

She gives him a high five. "We'd better get back. It's almost five." She tugs on my hand, pulling me back toward the carnival.

We take a few hurried steps through the parking lot. "It's so nice to see the two of you getting along, finally," Marnie says.

I just look at her.

"Ace has been so supersweet this year. I mean, he's always been one of my best friends, but since school started, it's been different. We tell each other everything," she says, standing on her tiptoes and kissing my cheek.

9

OCTOBER
Seven Months Before

"How'd you do on that calculus exam?" JC leans against my locker before first period.

"I have it right here. Take a look," I say, handing it to him and looking over the heads in the hallway for Marnie. She said she'd meet me here. She mentioned something about her mom taking her out for doughnuts this morning. Otherwise, I would have picked her up in my truck and brought her to school. This morning, it was just me and JC.

"Calculus, man. I really blew it," JC says, handing me back my A+ test paper. The buzzer sounds, and kids scatter into their homerooms. I still haven't seen Marnie.

I try to bite back my disappointment, but it's no use. I am disappointed. I really wanted to see her this morning.

When the five-minute warning buzzer for first period sounds, JC and I go our separate ways. I head toward the gym (What sucks more than PE first period of the day? Nothing.) and JC heads to a science lab.

"Catch you later," JC says, slapping me on the back. He's barely awake.

I try to stand on my tiptoes and peer over all the heads in the hallway. Where is Marnie? Why haven't I seen her yet? I pull my phone out of my pocket and surreptitiously send her a forbidden text.

Where RU?

I walk down the main hall on my way to PE, and I see Ace and Marnie walking toward me from the direction of the main office. Marnie has her hand around Ace's forearm. They are laughing together. My stomach burns.

"Marnie!" I call.

She drops her arm and waves to me. "Hi, Sam!" Ace noticeably grimaces.

"I thought we were meeting this morning," I say, grabbing for her hand and trying not to look at Ace.

"My mom and I ran into Ace at the doughnut shop. He offered to give me a ride. We're a little bit late. We just checked in at the office," she says, her smile wide.

"Why were you late?"

"Too many doughnuts, I guess." Marnie laughs.

"Yeah, too many doughnuts," Ace says, and they both

laugh together.

"I was waiting for you," I say, attempting to keep the whine out of my voice and failing miserably.

"I'm sorry. But I'm here now, right?" Marnie says and stands on her tiptoes for a kiss. I give her one right on the lips in front of Ace.

"Bye, Marn. I'm glad I ran into you this morning," Ace says.

"Thanks for the ride." She giggles.

Ace turns and walks down the hall, never acknowledging me at all.

"Funny that Ace was at the same doughnut shop as you, don't you think?" I say to Marnie.

"Yeah. Lucky too. I didn't have to ride with my mom."

"I don't really like you riding with Ace." Ever since Ace got his Jeep, Marnie rides with him at least once a week, usually more.

"Oh, for crying out loud, Sam. You can't tell me who I can and can't ride to school with," she says, rolling her eyes. "I thought you guys were getting along now. Ace never says anything bad about you." She pulls her hand from mine.

I stop walking. "Not to you he doesn't. You don't know what he's like when no one is around," I say.

Marnie stops walking too, and stares at me. "I don't even know what that means, Sam. You aren't making any sense."

I grit my teeth. "I have PE right now. I have to go the other way," I say, pointing over my shoulder toward the gym.

"Then I guess I'll see you," she says, her eyes narrowing. She turns on her heel and walks away.

"Yeah. I'll see you," I say to her back. I watch her for a minute, her hips swinging and her curls bouncing against her back.

I don't know how to make it clear. She can't see it. No one sees it but me, and I know I sound like a pussy whenever I try to explain.

I check the schedule outside the boys' locker room. Weight training this week. I take back what I said earlier about PE in the morning. Weight training first thing in the morning is so much worse. I look down the list of guys in the class with me.

Ace Quinn.

Of course.

So far, today sucks.

I dress quickly in the locker room in my wrinkled green PE shorts and Broadmeadow tank top and head for the weight room. Ace is already there with a bunch of other football players. They all laugh loudly when I walk in.

Coach Paul blows a whistle, and everyone quiets down a bit. "Seniors, here you are. Weight training. You've all done it. I don't need to repeat myself. Partner up and start lifting. Don't make me get up," he says, settling himself behind a desk with a magazine.

"Partners?" Ace taps me on the shoulder.

"Are you kidding me?" I say.

"Nah, come on. If Marnie's going to be your girlfriend, maybe we ought to make an effort," he says, making air quotes around the word "girlfriend."

I stare at him. He looks serious. I look around the weight room. Everyone else has partnered up and spread out among the weight benches. Ace and I seem to be the only two left without partners. I think about Marnie. She seemed so pissed off in the hallway just now.

"Quinn and North! What are you doing over there, the Texas two-step? Get moving!" Coach Paul shouts from the desk.

"What do you say?" Ace asks.

I stare at him for longer than I'm comfortable, but I can't look away. What's he hiding underneath that blank face? We're in the gym, surrounded by other people. Coaches. Football players. Surely he wouldn't be stupid enough to say something to me here.

"Did you enjoy your doughnut date?" I say, my voice low and shaking.

Ace blinks and his face changes. "Last time I checked, she didn't have a Property of Sam tattoo on her ass," he says, his eyes narrowing. "We're friends, North. I think you're going to have to get used to that."

"Quinn and North! Get started now, or take a zero for the day," Coach Paul yells from his chair.

"I'm making an effort here, Sam. You're the one who's being a jerk," Ace says, a smile dancing on his lips.

I look down. "She's mine. Don't forget that," I say to the floor.

"Uh-huh," he says, walking toward an empty bench in the corner. "You first. I'll spot."

"One-thirty," I say to him as he heads to the wall to grab weights for the bench.

"I got your back, Sam," he says.

I do a few push-ups on the wall to warm up my arms while Ace gets the weights ready.

"All set, champ. Let's see what you got," Ace calls when he's ready.

I lie down on the bench and exhale a few times before pushing up on the bar. It feels much heavier than one-thirty, but I don't question it. I haven't exactly been putting in my best effort in the weight room this football season. I must be really out of shape.

My arms start to shake under the weight after just a few presses. I exhale in puffs. "That's it. I'm done," I say to Ace between puffs.

Ace looks down at me struggling. "You can keep going. I added tens instead of fives. You're at one-forty here, rock star. You can keep going."

"I told you I can only do one-thirty," I manage to say.

"Keep going," Ace growls.

I slowly push the bar away from my chest, knowing I've only got one or two more pushes in me before this bar collapses on my throat.

"Something interesting happened to me and my dad the other day," Ace says, watching me struggle to push the bar up.

"Ace, I can't. Can you please help me get the bar up?" I push with all I've got, but my arms just shake.

"We were in the garage, and there was this cockroach. Every time I tried to step on it, it ran into a dark corner. My dad said, 'It thinks it's stronger than you are. Smarter. You've got to show it who is boss.'"

"Ace, please," I say, out of breath now.

"You've got to stomp on it and stomp on it and stomp on it until it knows who makes the rules," Ace says, picking at his fingernails and leaning against the bench.

I can barely push the bar off my chest.

"See, cockroaches like to hide when there's danger. They think they've outsmarted you. They think they have the upper hand. You've got to be tenacious. Consistent," he says, leaning against the weight bench.

"Just help me," I say, my face burning from the effort of lifting the bar away from my throat.

"There are some people that are like that too. Don't you think, Samantha? Cockroaches who think they can invade your house and then hide when you try to step on them. Yet every time you turn around, there they are taunting you.

Winning SAOTY. Fucking the girl you've liked for years. I've got news for that little cockroach. Next time he comes out of hiding to taunt me, I'll be waiting. It'll be the last time that roach hides in my garage," he says.

The bar slips closer and closer to my neck. Sweat is pouring down my forehead.

Ace bends down close to my ear, putting his hand on the bar. "I could push this bar right down on your throat, dickless. Be a man. Lift the fucking weights. Do it for Marnie," he whispers.

I push as hard as I can, but the bar barely moves. I close my eyes and try not to panic. I know if I'm not breathing right that I'll never get the weights off my chest. I open my eyes and see Coach Paul approaching behind Ace. My eyes widen. "Coach...Coach Pa..." I croak.

Ace grabs the bar with one hand and pulls it up to the rack quickly. "Don't say a word," he growls at me.

He has that look in his eye. I've seen it at least once before. When he hit me in the face with a hockey stick in fourth grade.

His mom must have heard me scream and ran outside.

"Don't say a word," he growled at me then.

"It was an accident, Mom! I swear!" He ran toward his mother.

She ran straight for me and held my chin in her hands, looking at the goose egg forming above my eye.

"We were playing, and Sam ran in front of me as I was

swinging at the puck. I swear!" He started crying, loudly, when his mother didn't look away from me. He even produced tears. That's when Mrs. Quinn let me go and turned to put an arm around Ace.

"You should watch where you're going when Ace has a hockey stick in his hand," Mrs. Quinn said, clucking her tongue. "You go home and let your mama check out that eye."

I ran home, blood dripping onto my T-shirt, and my mother took me to the emergency room. I got twelve stitches right below my eyebrow and had to wear a pirate patch on my left eye for almost three weeks.

"You boys okay?" Coach Paul asks. Ace gives me a look.

I stare back at him and then look down at the floor, rubbing the scar right below my eyebrow. "Just a little out of practice," I say.

Coach Paul looks at me for a few more seconds, but walks back to his desk without saying anything.

"Two-ten," Ace says. "Load 'em up." He points his chin toward the weight wall and settles himself on the bench.

He easily lifts my weights in hurried presses while I gather two 35-pound weights from the wall.

"I'm just warming up," he says slowly when I get back to the bench, a smirk curling his lip.

10

NOVEMBER
Six Months Before

"We say Broad, you say Meadow! Ready? BROAD—"

"MEADOW!" the crowd screams.

"I think this is my favorite thing about high school," JC yells in my ear next to me.

"Pep rallies?" I laugh, clapping along with the cheerleaders.

"Second only to watching Jeannie in that skirt, which I actually get to do at pep rallies, so…" JC says, motioning to the cheerleaders in front of us.

I watch the cheerleaders for a minute. Actually, I watch Marnie. She's right in the front, her curly ponytail high on her head. She turns her head like she can feel me watching her and catches my eye. A sly smile spreads across her face like she has a secret she only wants to share with me. She winks before turning back to the crowd, pom-poms flying. A few days after our fight about her doughnut date with Ace, she threw pebbles at my bedroom window again. We didn't go out, but I snuck her into my room. She stayed until the sunrise.

"Come on, pep rallies?" I laugh again, not able to take my eyes off Marnie.

JC raises his eyebrows as the marching band comes into the gym in full uniform, playing the Broadmeadow fight song. The crowd stands and claps and sings along.

"...with three cheers for BROOOOOAAAAADMeadow! Fight! Fight! Fight!" we all sing.

The principal, Dr. Davis, approaches the microphone and the cheerleaders stand behind him, kicking their legs to the side and shaking their pompoms for all they're worth.

"Are we ready to beat Plantation?" Dr. Davis yells into the microphone.

The crowd screams, and the football team stands up. We all pump our fists in unison like we practiced. Yes. We practiced for the pep rally. Grandpa made us.

"The school wants to see a united team, boys. When Dr. Davis asks if we are ready to beat Plantation, we are going to stand up and silently pump our fists in the air. It'll be a great effect, boys. Let's make the school proud," he told us last night after practice.

I'm surprised none of us forgot to stand and pump our fists. As stupid as I feel standing here pumping my fist in the air silently, I have to admit that Grandpa was right. The crowd is almost silent, and I can feel a thousand eyes on us. One by one, the student body joins in, pumping their fists in time with ours. The cheerleaders pump their pom-poms. My heart starts to beat faster, and I smile in spite of myself. I catch sight of JC next to me, and a smile is spreading across his face too. Maybe he's right. Maybe this is just a little bit cool.

"Let's all come out and support our Beavers at tonight's parade," Dr. Davis says, and the crowd erupts again. The cheerleaders spread a wide paper banner across the gym exit. In red paint, it reads: "Let's Go, BEAVERS! Beat those PANTHERS!" The team runs through the banner one at a time. JC and I are the last to go through, the crowd's cheers ringing in our ears.

We meet the rest of the team in the locker room. "We're meeting at Independence Park at five thirty, boys. The fire truck will be there. Remember, senior players on the fire truck only. The rest of you will walk behind the truck and throw candy. No funny business either. If I hear or see any-thing...you will not be playing in the game tomorrow morn-ing. I don't care who you are or what position you play. I'm not kidding. You all understand?" Grandpa asks, raising his eyebrows at us.

Most of us nod silently.

"Bring it in, Beavers," he says quietly, putting his hand in the middle of the huddle. "Win on three. One, two, three."

"WIN," we all say, breaking the huddle.

"Come on, agree with me. Pep rallies are one of the best things about high school," JC says as we walk out of the gym toward my truck in the senior lot.

"Yeah, alright. Maybe this year the pep rally wasn't so bad," I say.

We drive silently toward home, JC leaning back on the headrest, his eyes closed. I'm thinking about Marnie. That smile she gave me at the pep rally. That night I snuck her into my room. Those few days in school after that, when we found every opportunity to be alone. Under a staircase. In an empty classroom. Behind the field house.

"You're grinding your teeth, man. What are you thinking about?" JC asks me.

"Nothing. What are you thinking about?"

"Next year," he says, turning his head toward the window.

"What about it?"

"I don't know. Do you ever think about what it will be like? We've been staring at these same people for our entire lives. Thirteen years we've been sitting next to each other in a cafeteria, going to the same parties, sharing the same space, basically. I know when I walk into a classroom, I'll know most of the people in there," he says. "College. It's just going to be different."

"That's pretty deep for a Wednesday afternoon," I say.

"Shut up, butt nugget. I'm serious. Aren't you nervous?" he asks.

"About the game? It's not like we'll even get to play, JC—"

"No, not about the game!" He sighs loudly. "Just…Never mind."

"I guess I don't understand what you're getting at," I say. "Sure, we know that when we walk into Spanish class on Monday morning, the same cast of idiots will be sitting there. Whatever. Don't you think college will be an adventure, though? See new people? Talk about new things? You can be whoever you want to be. No one will know anything about you. You could almost reinvent yourself," I say, shrugging.

I pull the truck into JC's driveway. "Maybe I don't want to reinvent myself," he says, getting out and slamming the door.

"I'll see you in a few hours!" I yell out my open window.

JC just raises his right hand without turning around. He opens his front door and goes inside, his shoulders slumped forward.

I call Marnie as I back up out of JC's driveway. "I just had the strangest thing happen with JC," I say when she picks up.

"Tell me," she says.

"He got all quiet and started talking about how he won't know anyone in college. Then he didn't even say good-bye. He just slammed the door and slumped inside," I tell her.

"Maybe he's just worried about—"

Boop boop.

"Hang on. I've got another call coming in," she says.

Maybe she's right. Maybe he's just worried about college

or something. It seems weird. He's always talking about how ready he is to get out of Easthaven. Maybe now that it's getting closer, he's having second thoughts.

"Hey, I've got to take this. It's Ace," she says.

"Ace?" I say, trying to keep my voice even.

"Yeah, we're riding to the parade together tonight. We need to work out the details," she says.

"I can pick you up and bring you to the parade," I say.

"No, it's fine. Ace says he needs to talk to me about something anyway. I'll see you there, okay?" She hangs up before I can say anything else.

* * *

I pick JC up about ten minutes before we're supposed to be at the parade. He looks a little happier than he did a few hours ago. We're both wearing our away jerseys with our names on the back. I'm glad tomorrow's game is at Broadmeadow. We always do better at home.

"You boys be safe! Me and Dad will have our chairs set up outside the bakery!" JC's mom waves to us from their front porch.

"You feeling better?" I ask JC soon after he shuts his door.

"Sorry about that earlier," he says. "It just feels like every time there's an event or something, it's like a big reminder that this is the Last Time we're going to be doing it. I felt the same way during the carnival. This is our last Thanksgiving game against Plantation," he says, shrugging.

"It's only November, man. We've got plenty of our senior year left," I say.

JC just shrugs again. "I'm alright. I guess I just feel old," he says.

We drive the rest of the way to the school in silence. JC perks up when we park the truck, though, and we see Jeannie's parents dropping her off.

"James Christopher!" she squeals and then runs over to us.

"James Christopher?" I mumble, smirking.

"Hey, she can call me anything she wants as long as she keeps doing what she's doing. Hey, baby!" he says, picking her up in a big bear hug. Her cheerleader skirt rides up, and he puts his palm on her ass and squeezes.

She squeals and playfully swats at his hand. "Later," she says in his ear loudly enough for me to hear.

"Where's Marnie?" Jeannie says when JC puts her down.

"She's coming with Ace..." I say.

We all walk toward the football field, where a mass of students is putting the finishing touches on their parade floats. Every club in the school is represented, and all of the floats are football themed. The Foreign Language Club's float has a giant papier-mâché Beaver in a Broadmeadow jersey devouring a football player in a blue and silver uniform, Plantation's colors.

The Photography Club's float shows the front page of the *Easthaven Daily Chronicle*. The headline reads: "Broadmeadow

Shuts Down Plantation in Thanksgiving Day Football Blowout." All of the members of the Photo Club are dressed like newsboys. They have tiny football-shaped candies in baskets to throw to the crowd during the parade.

At the end of the lineup of floats is the fire truck. I feel a rush of excitement seeing it. I've been waiting since my freshman year to be able to ride on the truck during the parade. The senior cheerleaders get to ride with us.

I look over at JC, and he's not hiding his smile at all. "This is going to be so cool," he says, picking up his pace and heading right for the fire truck. "See? Aren't you going to miss this next year?"

I shrug. *Yeah. I probably will.*

Marnie and Ace are already at the truck when JC and I get there. Ace is leaning against the truck, talking softly to Marnie. She's staring up at him, a wide smile on her face.

"Hey," I say loudly as I walk over.

Marnie jumps a little, startled. "Hey…" she says slowly, her eyes drifting from Ace to me.

I put my arm around her waist and pull her close for a kiss. She pulls back a little bit and rolls her eyes. "Be careful of my hair," she says. Her eyes blink over to Ace for less than a second, but I notice.

I let her go.

"Alright, Beavers!" Grandpa has a bullhorn. "Let's get settled. Seniors on the truck. Everyone else, grab a candy basket from the boosters," he says, motioning to the table of moms behind him.

Marnie is standing close, her arms folded across her chest. I take a step closer so that my arm touches hers. She flinches just slightly, but enough for me to notice. She takes a half step away.

"You okay?" I ask her.

She turns to me with a big smile. "Of course!" she says. I've seen that smile before. It's her cheerleader smile. It's bright and lights up her eyes. Her cheeks turn pink, and she has two dimples. It's completely fake. Her real smile is crooked and reveals only one dimple. Even when she's laughing so hard that she'll have a sore stomach the next day, her real smile only produces one dimple. I asked her once how that was possible.

"It's a cheerleader smile," she explained. "I can turn it on like a lamp. Years of practice. We have to smile through an entire game, even if we're losing by a hundred points. It's ridiculous, but we actually have to practice smiling."

"Are you going to sit with me on the truck?" I ask her, trying again to get close. I shift my weight toward her, and my jersey just brushes against her arm.

She takes another half step away. "Cheerleaders are walking this year," she says, looking at the ground. "I'll catch up with you at the end of the parade." She leans toward me and kisses my cheek. Well, almost. She missed.

And then she's gone, leaving in her wake the memory of the two-dimpled cheerleader smile and the smell of spearmint gum.

The cheerleaders are right in front of the fire truck this year. I sit as close as I can to the front of the truck. JC settles in next to me, as wiggly as a kid who has eaten an entire birthday cake. "I've been waiting four years to ride in the parade like this. This is so cool," he says.

"Did you notice Marnie and Ace when we got here?" I ask him.

"Nah," he replies, still smiling from ear to ear. His eyes are shining in the dim light of the park.

"They looked awfully close," I say.

"Are you ever going to let that go? It's our senior year, man. Just get through it, and you'll never have to see him again. Jeez, Sam. Are you capable of enjoying anything?" he asks.

"Yeah, but—"

"But nothing," JC interrupts. "Marnie and Ace have been friends for years. Let that shit go. Are you guys even officially, like, a thing?"

"What's that supposed to mean?" I ask, sitting up straighter. A thing? Of course we're a thing. Most of the time. Some of the time. We're definitely something.

The fire truck starts to move, and the team lets out a big cheer. I don't feel like I can join in.

"Seriously. What do you mean, 'a thing'?" I poke JC's arm.

"Just have fun! Stop worrying about all that. Quit thinking about Ace all the time," JC says, then lets out a giant whoop as the fire truck turns the corner onto the parade route.

"I can't. You don't understand. You don't see it. Nobody sees it," I say, but JC isn't listening anymore. The crowd is cheering and waving at us, and most of the team is waving back. I catch sight of Ace at the very front of the truck. He's waving and smiling like the Mayor of Easthaven, but he's not watching the crowd. I follow his line of sight.

He's watching Marnie.

I watch Marnie.

She throws a look over her shoulder, but not at me.

The parade winds through Easthaven and ends back at Independence Park, where a bonfire is roaring when we arrive. The seniors hop down from the fire truck and are met with raucous applause from the audience that has gathered around the fire. Mostly Broadmeadow alumni, coming back to Easthaven to relive their Beaver glory days. Grandpa grabs the bullhorn again.

"Thank you, Easthaven!" he says. More crazy applause.

"Don't forget to come out and support our boys tomorrow morning. Are we going to beat those Panthers?" he asks, then puts his hand to his ear.

The crowd whoops and claps in response.

"That's what I like to hear!" he says.

I find Marnie by the fire, alone. "Hey," I say, coming up next to her.

"I'm sorry about before," she says, stepping closer to me.

"Do you want to talk about it?"

"Just home stuff," she says.

"I'm here if you want to say more," I tell her, running my fingers down her arm and reaching for her hand.

"My parents aren't getting along. It'll be fine, I'm sure, but I hate listening to them argue," she says, letting me take her hand. She squeezes my fingers.

I try to remember a time when my own parents argued loudly enough for me to hear, but I can't pretend to know what that's like.

"I'm sorry," I say.

Marnie shrugs. "It'll be fine," she says dismissively. "I think it's just what parents do."

I don't know what else to say, so I squeeze her hand. I hope that it's enough.

We start wandering. Like you do when you're comfortable with someone and you feel safe. We wander away from the bonfire and toward the playground. When we get there, Marnie plops down on a hard plastic swing. I stand behind her and start pushing.

"Being a senior isn't exactly what I thought it was going to be," she says quietly.

"What do you mean?"

Marnie sighs. "I don't know. I thought it would be more fun, but there's, like, all this stuff we have to do. So much that's expected of us. I just feel like…like everyone is already expecting us to be completely grown up," she says.

"Your parents?"

"Everyone, Sam. Yeah, my parents. But also teachers and coaches and just...everyone. I have heard so many times this year 'You're a senior now. You can't just goof off anymore' from so many people. I don't know. I feel like I want more time to be irresponsible or something. It's all happening too fast. Don't listen to me. I don't know what I'm talking about," she says.

"No, I understand," I say, even though I don't exactly understand.

"Sorry I'm being a downer," she says.

"You're not a downer, Marn. It's okay if we talk like this. You don't always have to be Little Miss Sunshine," I say.

"I was talking with Ace on the way here earlier. He said almost the same thing," she says.

"Did he really? Huh," I say, gritting my teeth.

"He's been such a good friend this year. He's always right there. It's been nice," she says, smiling softly.

"Are you saying I'm not always right there?"

"It's not a competition, Sam," she says, jumping off the swing. Her little cheerleader skirt flies up and reveals blue trunks she wears underneath.

Marnie starts walking deeper into the woods. I walk quickly to keep up. "I know it's not," I say. "But seriously, aren't I there for you too?"

Marnie sighs. "Yes, Sam, you're there for me too," she sing-songs and rolls her eyes.

Suddenly Marnie stops walking and pushes my back into a tree, kissing me hard on the lips. She hooks her fingers just inside the waistband of my jeans.

"What's this for?" I ask her while she kisses my neck.

"Must be the chill in the air," she says, giggling.

I kiss her back, my hands finding the curve of her hip and pulling her as close to me as I can. She puts her hands inside my jacket, and her fingers travel down my chest to my stomach. She kisses my neck.

"Hey," I whisper to her. "JC just asked me if we were 'a thing,'" I say.

"Mmm," she says, her lips still on my neck.

"I didn't know what to tell him," I say. "I mean, I say we're a thing. We're together...most of the time. It's definitely a thing, isn't it? We're a thing," I say.

"Why do you feel like you need to define it all the time?" she asks, her hands still on my stomach, her pinkies tracing little circles.

"I-I don't," I stammer, lying through my teeth.

"We're just having fun," she says, her hands traveling down. "Aren't you having fun?" she asks, her lips and teeth back on my neck and ear.

"Yeah, I'm definitely having fun. But I just...I want you to be my girlfriend, Marn," I say, trying not to think about her hands rubbing the outside of my thighs right now.

"I don't think we need to label this, Sam. We're doing

what feels good, right?" she says, squeezing her hands low on my hips.

"Yeah, but—"

"Sam. Stop it," she says, backing away from me and putting her hands on her own waist.

"Why can't we just say you're my girlfriend? I mean, you are, right?" I say, trying to reach for her hands again.

"Let's just go back to the fire," she says, keeping her hands on her waist and stomping back through the woods toward the glow of the bonfire.

I follow behind her, trying to figure out when the conversation went off the rails. Marnie disappears as soon as we get close to the party. I find JC and Jeannie near the hot chocolate table.

"Where's Marnie?" Jeannie asks.

"I don't…uh…She went that way," I say, pointing to the fire.

Jeannie stands on her tiptoes and kisses JC on the cheek. "I'll see you in a bit, James Christopher," she says.

"Marnie's being weird," I say to JC when Jeannie jogs off.

I tell him the whole weird conversation I had with Marnie at the swings. "And she's spending an awful lot of time with Ace. I don't know what that means, but I know I don't like it," I say, pulling a cup of steaming hot chocolate from the table.

"I think you spend too much time worrying about Ace.

Just go with it. If Marnie doesn't want to define anything but she's still happy to be with you, than so be it. If you want her, you may just have to get used to having Ace around," JC says, shrugging.

"Psh" is the only answer I have for that.

A few minutes later, the king of assholes himself saunters up to us. "What's up, girls? Marnie wanted me to tell you that I'm bringing her home tonight," he says, tapping my shoulder.

"But...why?" I ask.

"I don't know," he says, smirking at me and raising his eyebrows. "She asked me for a ride. I said yes. She asked me to come tell you. I said yes. That's all I know," he says. His eyes narrow at me, and his lip curls into a tiny smile.

"Okay...why didn't she tell me herself?" I ask Ace.

"Hey, Jeannie's waving at me. I'll be right back," JC says, throwing his paper cup in the trash can and jogging away.

"All I know is that she came out of the woods all sobby and whiny and asked me to take her home. You must have really pissed her off. What did you do, show her that you're dickless?" Ace asks, crossing his arms across his chest.

I ignore him and crumple my paper cup in my fist.

"Have a good night with Rosie Palm, Samantha," he says, grabbing his crotch and walking away backwards.

"Hey!" I yell with more force than I feel.

Ace walks slowly back toward me, his hand still firmly planted on his crotch.

"Yes?" he says when he reaches me. He stands an inch or two from my face, his head cocked to the side.

"Don't..." I say, my voice shaking. My insides have turned to ice, and I can barely breathe in or out with him standing that close to me.

"Don't what, Samantha? Don't touch your girlfriend? Aww, I would never do that unless she asked me to. Begged me. Sat right down and demanded. But remember what I said to you. QB2 never gets the girl in the end," he says, squeezing his palm around his crotch and groaning.

He walks away toward the parking lot, and I'm left standing alone, the ice in my gut keeping me frozen to this space. My breath comes in ragged chops, and my hands are shaking.

You're not twelve years old anymore, Sam.

11

DECEMBER
Five Months Before

We won our Thanksgiving game against Plantation, but lost in the playoff round that would have sent us to state. Ace made a bad pass during the last play of the game, and we lost 36–35. It was gut-wrenching, but I was kind of glad the season was over. That meant it was finally basketball season, and basketball season meant no Ace. The day after that loss, the temperature hovered around 33 degrees and rain was falling at a steady clip. I could hear the angry ocean just outside my window, but there was another noise too. A slapping sound, like heavy boots clomping around in puddles.

It was still dark outside when I peeked through the blinds and saw Mr. Quinn standing in his driveway holding an umbrella and a stopwatch. He was yelling something toward the street, but I couldn't hear what he was saying. I pulled the blinds up slightly and saw Ace in his football shorts and jersey, running suicides in the cul-de-sac. He was soaking wet, but running those suicides at a terrifyingly fast pace. I flipped the lock on my window and raised it up a little bit. I could hear Mr. Quinn's voice yelling through the rain.

"Drive! Drive! Drive! Not going to throw a pass like that and become a Longhorn, are you?"

Ace's voice answered back, out of breath and shaking but still loud, "No, sir!"

"Not going to be beat by some pussy, are you? No son of mine comes in second, does he?"

"No, sir!"

I closed my window and locked it again.

* * *

It's the third week of basketball practice, and I am sucking air like a flat tire. Coach has us running laps until our faces turn purple and we can barely stand up, never mind talk to each other.

"If you can quit yappin' to each other...quit flappin' yer gums...maybe we can win a championship this year. Right, North?" he says, clapping me on the back way harder than is necessary.

I look at JC. He's hunched over by the garbage can. I know he's just hurled.

"One more lap, boys, and then we scrimmage," he shouts at us.

The whistle blows, and we all take off from the baseline. Suicides.

When practice is over, I bring JC home. He looks a little green.

"You okay, man? You look like shit," I tell him when we reach his driveway.

"Feeling it today. Jeannie's been over every night. I can't take these workouts every afternoon and every night," JC says, smirking.

"Shut up, buttlicker," I tell him.

"I'm gonna go take a nap before she gets here," he says, slamming the door to the truck.

Three days after Marnie drove off with Ace after the bonfire, she was at my window again. We walked down to the beach in the dark, bundled up in heavy coats and scarves and mittens. I thought about what JC said about "just going with it." I told Marnie I was sorry for pushing her for a relationship definition, and she apologized for getting mad at me and stomping off. We crawled up into a lifeguard chair for a couple of hours after that.

Now that basketball season has started, we're back to catching quick minutes alone in our secret spots at school. As much as I hate not knowing when I'll be with her again, the not knowing makes the school day a lot more exciting. A shared glance in the hallway sometimes means I can meet her in the back of the library by the foreign language dictionaries for a few minutes between PE and chemistry.

When I get home from practice, Mom is there, poring over some paperwork at the kitchen counter. Dad's blue robe is next to her on the counter. Her pill bottle is next to it.

"Hi, honey, how was your practice?" she asks, not looking up from behind her reading glasses.

"Exhausting," I say, grabbing the orange juice from the fridge and gulping it straight from the carton. She hates it when I do that.

"I hate it when you do that, Sam," she says, pulling a glass from the cabinet behind her and handing it to me. I go upstairs to shower and change and then flop on the couch with my English lit text. Mom has moved to the sunroom and is doing her nightly yoga routine. The sun is streaming in through the back windows, and Edgar Allan Poe is putting me to sleep on the couch. I almost hit myself in the face with my lit book at least six times before I hear the doorbell.

"Can you get that, Sam? I'm right in the middle of this..." Mom yells.

I get up from the couch and glance back toward the sunroom. Mom is on her stomach, and her knees are bent at a really scary angle. "Frog pose!" She smiles at me.

I answer the door, shaking my head.

Ace.

"Oh...hi, Sam," he says, with a great big smile on his face, glancing behind me into the house. "Where's your mom?" he asks.

"Busy," I say, arms stiffening on the door handle.

"My mom asked me to come over and borrow yesterday's paper. She said your mom knew I was coming," Ace says, his smile disappearing.

"Oh…well…let me go get it, I guess," I say, not wanting to turn my back on him.

I walk into the kitchen to the bin where I know Mom keeps the old newspapers until she has a chance to go by the recycling center.

"So, Sam. Everything good with Marnie?" Ace asks, sitting down at a stool in the kitchen and picking up an apple from the fruit bowl.

"Yeah, why wouldn't it be?" I say, rifling through the old newspapers in the stack.

"I don't know," he says, taking a big bite of the apple. "I saw Marnie yesterday," he says.

"Yeah?" I say, trying not to care but failing miserably. I want to hit him. Grab him by the neck. Tell him to go to hell.

"Yeah. She says you've been so busy at basketball that you haven't had much time for her lately. I think she's lonely," he says, biting into the apple again. I can feel his eyes on my back.

"She's not lonely. I have plenty of time for her," I say, barely keeping the edge out of my voice.

"Mmm. So sure about that, Samantha?" he says, throwing something onto the table.

"What is that?" I ask him, standing up.

"Take a look," he says, a smirk spreading across his smarmy face while he sinks his teeth into the apple again.

It's a condom wrapper. Open and empty.

"Found it in Marnie's room. Now I know it doesn't belong to you, dickless. She's got someone else taking care of business while you play basketball with those d-bag idiots," he says.

"Fuck you, Ace. Fuck you. You're lying," I say through my teeth. I glance toward the sunroom, where my mother is still completely involved in her yoga poses. "Get out of my house," I say, throwing the wrapper at his chest.

"I'm not lying, dickless. She's not sleeping with you because she's sleeping with someone else. Get it through that thick head of yours. She's not into you. She's with you out of pity. A fatherless, dickless d-bag? Oh yeah, you've got the sympathy vote, Samantha," he says, standing up.

He leaves the apple, half eaten and browning, sitting on the kitchen counter and saunters toward the front door, yesterday's newspaper tucked up under his arm.

"You're an asshole, Ace. Shut up about Marnie. You don't know what you're talking about," I say to his back, following him to the front door.

"Ace! What a nice surprise! Did Sam find the paper your mother wanted?" My mother appears behind me, sweating with a towel around her neck.

"Mrs. North! How nice to see you again," Ace leans past me and plants a kiss on my mother's cheek, his hand shoving the condom wrapper back into his pocket. "I was just telling Sam here, good luck at this weekend's basketball game! I know it's an important one. Plantation High is a tough opponent. Right, Sam? I'll be out of your way now, ma'am. It was so nice to see you again. Don't be a stranger," Ace says to my mom, holding out his hand. His oily smile spreads across his face, and he looks like a crocodile about to bite.

I slam the door shut as soon as his foot hits the porch.

"Such a nice kid, that Ace. I don't know why the two of you aren't better friends," my mom mutters as she makes her way back to the kitchen. "Sam, why can't you ever throw anything away?" she asks, holding Ace's half-eaten apple in her hand.

* * *

I raise the gun from my hip and pop off two shots before lowering it back down. Two perfect shots, one right between the eyes of the human-shaped target and one in the chest. I glance over at Grandpa as I lay the gun down on the carpeted countertop. He motions to me to take the earmuffs off.

"Nice job. That's what I was talking about. You've got to be able to take care of yourself. It's all about safety, Sam." He claps me on the back. "How many bullets you got left in the case? You want to keep shooting or pack it up?"

"I can finish what's in the case. You can start packing up the truck if you want. I'm good by myself," I say.

Grandpa knits his eyebrows. "You sure?"

I nod and smile.

He shrugs and loads his gun into the case while I reposition my green earmuffs. I pull the target toward me and pull it off the clips. I'm saving this one. I fold it up and put it in the gun case. I pull out another human-shaped target and clip it to the string. Grandpa Carl didn't ask any questions when I asked him to pick me up a package of them. He just smiled and clapped me on the back.

I load my last six bullets into the chamber and click it closed. Lower the gun to my hip and put my finger on the trigger. The cool steel rubs my pointer finger, and my palm squeezes against the rubber grip. I look down at my feet. Close my eyes.

"She's got someone else taking care of business," he said.

Pop. In the gut.

"She's not that into you," he said.

Pop. In the neck.

"A fatherless, dickless d-bag," he called me.

Pop. Between the eyes.

"You've got the sympathy vote, Samantha."

PopPopPop.

In the chest. In the chest. In the chest.

As soon as I bury those six bullets in the target, I can take a deep breath again. Some of the steam from this morning has been let out of the pot. I lay the gun back down on the carpeted counter. Snap open the chamber and check to make sure there are no more bullets left. I pack the gun and my earmuffs into the bag and pull the target toward me. I unclip it from the string and take a pencil out of my equipment bag.

I write the date in miniscule print on the bottom of the target. I quickly fold the target and throw it in the bottom of the bag just as Grandpa opens the door.

"Ready, kiddo? I was watching that last round on the TV out there. Nice job! You been practicing without me?" he says.

I just smile.

"You ready for tonight?" Grandpa asks me when we get back in the car. "Kind of a big game, isn't it?"

"I'm ready now, Grandpa," I say. Plantation High School's basketball team is ranked number one in the state, but we're just two spots behind them in the standings. If we can win this one game, we have a real solid chance at going to the state championship.

"What time do you have to be there? Do you want me to bring you?" he asks as we pull into the driveway.

"Nah, I gotta pick up JC and everything. I'll see you at the game, though, right?"

"Wouldn't miss it, kiddo," he says, smiling at me. "Hey, you did real good today. I'm proud of you. Glad you're finally taking this seriously," he says.

I pick up JC about an hour later, and we head to the school. He is jumpy as hell in the passenger seat of the truck.

"What's with you?" I ask him.

"Freaking out, man. This game...this game." He shakes his head.

"It's just like any other game. Plus it's at home. You'll be fine. We'll be fine," I say.

"Scouts. Scouts will be all over this game. Coach O told me that UConn and UMass are coming out. What if he doesn't put me in? Or worse, what if he does put me in and I fall on my ass? Then what?" he asks, wringing his hands.

"Well...then...then you'll get up off your ass and try again. Right? Just play it like it's a normal game. It's going to be fine, JC," I say.

"Easy for you to say, superstar. You've got the SAOTY award. They'll all be looking at you whether you fall on your ass or not. I've got about a snowball's chance in hell of playing at UConn," he says, all moody and broody.

"Look, play the low post. Plantation's got that sophomore guy, what's-his-name, playing down there. He's shorter than you, and he never guards outside the key. Lay off the boards and back up to three-point land. He won't touch you out there, and you know you can make that shot all day long. I'll feed you the ball a couple of times, and you'll be golden. Just stay on his side, all right?"

JC nods all quick, but still looks like he's going to throw up. "Hey, JC," I say.

He turns to me.

"We got this," I say, knocking knuckles with him.

The game is almost wrapped up. We've been ahead for three quarters, which is unheard of against this year's Plantation team. What's-his-name, low-post guy, turns out to be Marcus Wilson, this sophomore phenom that Plantation picked up from some private school at the beginning of the season. He's all anyone has been talking about this season, but I'm not really impressed. The kid can shoot, but he's not worth shit on defense. I've been feeding JC all night in three-point land, and he's sunk basket after basket.

"North, you're out. Let's get some of our young guys in there. We're up by fourteen...Now's the time. JC, stay in. Keep playing low, stay out of the key. Let's go boys," Coach O tells us before the fourth quarter.

I park myself on the bench next to Coach O to watch JC take over the fourth quarter. I suck water from my squirt bottle and look at Marnie. She's in the back row of cheerleaders. She's kneeling on the sidelines and giggling with Ace. He and his cronies have set up camp right behind the cheerleaders. Marnie sees me watching her, and she waves with a big smile. I lift my chin and smile at her.

Plantation is mopping the floor with our young guys, but JC is holding his own. He's trying to keep the team together out there, but these guys are just too nervous. JC calls a play, and the point guard gets confused and trips over his own shoes. Turnover number one. Marcus Wilson scores two before JC can make it back down court. Full-court press. Wilson steals and scores again before we even get the ball past half-court.

Again and again, Broadmeadow loses the ball. I can see

JC sucking air out there, and I know he's doing all he can. The bench is on our feet now, screaming at our teammates and trying to turn this game back around. I look at Coach O, wondering how long he's going to let this go on. His face is purple and he's yelling. I'm worried he's going to blow a gasket. Why doesn't he just put us back in? Broadmeadow is now down by seven.

Finally he calls a time-out. Three minutes left to go. He pulls everyone but JC out and puts the rest of the first string back in. I'm rested now and ready for a fight. I glance over at Marnie. She's cheering, pom-poms flying. Ace is directly behind her. He sees me watching him and stands up behind Marnie, grinding his hips into the air right behind her.

I grit my teeth. I'm ready.

The ref blows the whistle, and JC inbounds the ball to me and takes off down court, setting up the low post and trying to tease Marcus Wilson out of his spot in the key. I see JC's lips moving, and I know he's talking smack. Wilson isn't having it, though, and he stays put, bouncing all over the place right inside the key. Why does everyone think this kid is so hot? I watch JC follow Marcus toward the key and then quickly backtrack as I give the signal for a play. He pulls back to the three-point line just as I heave a nice high pass his way. *Swoosh.* Now we're only down by four.

I give the signal for a full-court press as Plantation attempts to inbound the ball. JC defends the inbounder and I stand by

Wilson, ready to steal any pass that may come his way. JC jumps at just the right moment as the inbounder attempts to pass the ball, blocking it and tipping it backward to my waiting hands. Seeing an open shot, I go in for the layup, right over Marcus Wilson's head. *Boom.* Broadmeadow down by two.

I glance at the clock. One fifteen left. I pull the team back on defense, but yell to JC to hang back at half-court. "Be ready for the rebound pass," I tell him and then hold up three fingers.

JC nods. He knows what I mean.

Marcus Wilson has the ball, and he's moving slowly. He knows that if he runs down the shot clock, Broadmeadow will have to rush to score and Plantation will have a better chance at keeping their spotless record for the year. I decide to let him play for awhile. Let him get comfortable, a little lazy, and a little careless. I make a few fake attempts at stealing, and Wilson smiles at me.

"Gonna have to try harder than that, number 44," he says, dribbling right in my face.

I know I've got him good and worked up now. He's trying to push for the basket because the shot clock is running down. I'm on him like white on rice, and he can't get anywhere near the basket. I know my team is doing their job because he can't find an open pass either. His eyes go wild for a minute when he glances up at the shot clock, and I know he's going to make his move. I back up an inch or two, stand straight up, plant my feet, and clasp my hands together.

Marcus Wilson lowers his shoulder and comes charging at me, and I fall down on my backside.

Whistles blow, and the ref points his finger at Wilson. "Number 23! Charging! Broadmeadow ball!"

I jump up from the floor and run to the sideline, grabbing the ball from the ref. Before the Plantation team has time to recover, I toss the ball down to JC, who has set up perfectly, all alone at the other end of the court, just outside the three-point line. He catches the pass, bends at the knees, and sets up his perfect shot.

The crowd counts "4...3...2..." as JC lets the ball sail out of his hands in a perfect arc.

The whole court is silent as we watch JC's shot bounce on the rim once...twice...three times before it finally falls into the basket.

Broadmeadow wins by one. And JC is the hero. The team and I carry him out of the gym on our shoulders and Jeannie follows behind, her pom-poms and her ponytail bouncing along with her.

I glance behind me. Marcus Wilson is sitting in the middle of the gym floor. Crying.

It is decided in the locker room that tonight is worthy of a winter bonfire. The team quickly showers and changes, and we all text our girlfriends and other friends to meet us at East Beach in an hour. I call my mom and Grandpa and tell them the team's having a party and not to wait up.

The win tonight makes me feel invincible. Nothing can drag this night down. Nothing.

By the time the team gets to East Beach, the bonfire is raging and there is a crowd of kids gathered around.

I spot Marnie and Jeannie together right in the thick of things and drag JC over to them.

"The hero of Broadmeadow has arrived!" Jeannie shouts, and a whoop goes up in the crowd. Everyone claps, and JC's face turns bright purple.

I kiss Marnie on the cheek and grab her hand. "Let's take a walk," I say, showing her the big, fluffy blanket I have under my arm.

She blinks, and her smile disappears briefly. She looks back at the bonfire, and I see the muscles in her cheek twitch a little bit.

"Come on, Marn," I say, squeezing her hand.

She tilts her head to the side and looks at me, but doesn't move her feet. She turns back toward the fire, and her eyes scan the crowd. She puts a thumbnail in her mouth before she turns back to me. "Okay," she says.

I hold her gloved hand in mine and we walk along the shore, shivering a little bit. When we get farther away from the bonfire, I pull her toward the abandoned lifeguard stand. We climb up into the tall chair, and I wrap the giant blanket around both of us.

"Are you warm enough?" I ask her through chattering teeth.

"I feel okay," she says, turning her head toward me.

I kiss her, hard. She kisses me back for a minute and then puts her hand on my chest and pushes me back.

"What's the matter?" I ask.

"Nothing. I just don't feel like doing this right now," she says, tugging at the fingers of her gloves and avoiding my gaze. She lets out a frustrated sigh.

"Are you okay?" I ask.

"Why do you need to know if I'm okay? Because I don't feel like making out? Jeez, Sam," she says.

"No, I just...I thought you wanted to." I lean back in the chair.

She sighs loudly next to me and looks away.

"Hey," I say softly, touching her knee. "What's going on?"

"Just...nothing," she says.

The adrenaline from our win has all but disappeared now. I am sitting alone in the lifeguard chair, even though Marnie's thigh is only a centimeter away from my own. I gently take her hand in mine and hold it, my thumb tracing her knuckles. I consider it a good sign that she doesn't pull her hand away.

"Whatever is going on, you know you can tell me, right?" I say.

She shifts just slightly, and now her thigh is at least an inch away from my own. "Nothing's going on," she says, an edge creeping into her voice.

I watch the angry December ocean and feel like Marnie

is a million miles away. Her hand is limp in mine, and her other arm is still folded tightly across her middle. I squeeze her hand a little bit and wait for her to squeeze back. She doesn't. Instead, she just exhales loudly through her nose.

"Let's just go back and be with our friends," she says, pulling her hand from mine and climbing down from the chair without me.

I watch her jog back to the bonfire, the frog eyes on her hat bobbing along in the darkness. I'm not even sure what happened. I sit in the chair alone for a long time, trying to figure out where I made a mistake. Was I too pushy? I stopped when she wanted me to. I asked her what was wrong. I told her she could talk to me.

I sit alone long enough to notice that the crowd is starting to thin out. The fire is dying down slowly, and I see a few kids walking toward the ocean with buckets, ready to fill them up with sea water and pour it on the dying embers.

I climb down from the chair slowly and make my way back to the party. I am about two hundred yards from the parking lot when I spot Ace hugging a girl by his Jeep. His back is to me, and he has his arms wrapped tightly around a small form. His giant frame nearly swallows this poor girl, and I can't tell who it is from a distance. He pulls out of the hug and puts his hand on the girl's shoulder, and then gathers her in his arms again, rubbing her back with his palm. A sliver of green knitted cap is visible near his arm. A frog eye bobs about near his shoulder. The two climb into Ace's Jeep and drive away from the party.

I get a text from Marnie just a moment later. Getting a ride with a friend. See you tomorrow.

JANUARY
Four Months Before

I hardly see Marnie anymore. Things are just slightly south of okay. She never sneaks out at night to visit me anymore. At first I thought it was because it was too cold, or because we were both too busy. But she doesn't call or text anymore either. Sometimes she doesn't answer if I call or text her. She doesn't really look for me at school like she used to; we don't ever sit together at lunch anymore; and she rides to school with Ace instead of me almost every day. Maybe those seem like small, dumb things, but I want to fix it. I know she'll come back if I can just figure out how to fix it. She loves me.

I have plenty of time to think about it during conditioning drills at practice. Coach O'Hara keeps us running for at least half of every practice. That's a lot of freaking running.

"Running is 99 percent of this game, boys. Hustle. We can't always win games based on talent, but we can always outhustle. Let's move. Put some fire in your shoes, boys!" Coach O shouts from the bleachers while the team runs up and down, up and down, up and down the court a million times.

"I'm dying," JC says to me during a water break.

"Just keep up. You don't have to be the fastest guy out there," I say, letting him in on my strategy for making it through the endless drills.

"Easy for you to say, coach's pet," JC says, sweat dripping down the front of his practice jersey. He punches me in the arm and smiles.

"North! Come here, son. There's someone I need you to meet," Coach O'Hara calls to me.

I look up to see a tall man in a blue polo shirt talking to Coach O. I swipe at my dripping forehead with my wristband and jog over. As I get closer, I see "Oceanside College" stitched into the left shoulder of the tall man's polo shirt. My heart beats faster.

"Sam North, I'd like you to meet Coach Paul Dinsmoore," Coach O says.

I hold out my hand. "Nice to meet you, Coach Dinsmoore."

"The pleasure is all mine, Sam," he says, motioning to the bleachers. "Can we talk?"

My heart is beating out of my chest while Coach Dinsmoore talks about the kind of basketball program he's trying to build at Oceanside. He goes on and on about the new gymnasium that alumni funds have paid for and the kind of perks being an Oceanside player would come with, and touches on the kind of academic footing a degree from Oceanside would give me.

"Have you thought about Oceanside, Sam? You would be close to home," he says.

"I have thought about it," I tell him. "Both of my parents are...were...are alums."

"Is that right? Why don't you come spend a weekend with us? I'll hook you up with one of our best players. Come see what our program is all about," he says, standing up from the bleachers and holding out his hand again.

"I'd love that," I say.

"I'll leave the details with Coach O'Hara. Looking good out there, Sam. Keep up the good work," he says, smiling again.

"Thank you, sir," I say, smiling.

I jog back to the team with a little spring in my step. My sprints are faster, and I'm doing more than just keeping up now.

"He wants me to visit. Spend the weekend," I say to JC.

"That's awesome," he says between gasps.

I run and let my mind wander again. I'd be going to the same school as my dad. Taking classes in the same buildings he took classes in. Living in the dorms just like he did. I start to picture myself there, running sprints with the basketball team in the new gym. I know he'd be proud of me.

I leave practice with a huge smile on my face.

"Marnie has called the house three times in the last hour," Mom says when I walk in the door. She hands me the cordless phone.

"Why didn't she call my cell?" I say, taking it out of my pocket and checking the missed call log. Nothing from Marnie.

"She said she knew you were at practice and didn't want to disturb you," Mom says, her lips pulling into a smirk.

"Sorry, Mom."

"I had a client earlier...We were meditating," she says.

"I'll go call her back," I say, taking the phone from her and putting it back in its cradle on the wall. "I'll use my cell."

I run up to my room and drop my bag on the floor on top of a pile of dirty laundry. I sweep my arm over the bed and push the books and papers onto the floor before plopping down on my back and pulling out my phone and calling Marnie.

"Hey, you okay?" I say as soon as she picks up.

"Can we talk? Like in person?" she asks.

"Of course," I say.

"I'll be there in fifteen minutes," she says, hanging up. She didn't even say good-bye.

I jump into the shower and try to clean up as fast as I can. With a towel wrapped around my waist, I push all the junk on the floor under my bed and into my closet. I hear the doorbell ringing and Mom talking to Marnie before I even have time to pull on a pair of sweatpants.

There's a soft knock on my bedroom door. I'm still shirtless, but at least I have pants on.

"Hey," I say, opening the door and holding my arms open for a hug.

Marnie lets me hug her, but she pats my back. *Friend zone. Friend zone!* JC's voice echoes in my head.

"This coach from Oceanside came to practice today and invited me to spend the weekend there observing the basketball team. Isn't that awesome?"

"Yeah," Marnie says, pulling out of the hug and sitting down in my wooden desk chair.

"What's up, Marn? You okay?" I ask, pulling a sweatshirt from my bottom drawer.

"I think we should take a break," Marnie says, cutting right to the chase.

"What? Why?"

"I just don't feel like this is going anywhere anymore."

"What do you mean?"

"We shouldn't be doing this thing anymore, Sam. We want different things," she says, picking at a piece of lint on her pant leg.

"I don't understand. How do we want different things?"

She shrugs. "We just do. I don't know. I can't explain it. We're just not good together anymore," she says.

"But we can be," I say softly. "We just need to spend more time together. Once basketball season ends—"

"No, Sam. I'm saying this is over," she says quietly.

"I can be better. We just need time. I can show you. We can work on it—"

"No, I think it's best if we're just not together anymore," she says, still not looking at my face. "I have to go now," she says, but doesn't move from the chair.

I just look at her. Her curls are creeping out of her ponytail and framing her face. I want to reach out and push them gently behind her ear. Touch her skin. The hollow spot where her shoulder meets her neck. I want to make her laugh again. Quote song lyrics at her. See her crooked smile with one dimple.

She stands up from the chair suddenly and turns toward the door.

"Wait!" I say.

She turns to look at me, but her eyes never meet mine.

"Why are you doing this? You love me," I say, realizing how pathetic I sound after the words are already out.

Her lips tighten.

"Can I have a hug? Are we still...Can we still be friends?" I say it, but it feels weird coming out of my mouth. *Friends.*

I reach for her and gather her in a hug that she doesn't return.

"I really have to go," she says, pulling out of the hug.

"But—"

"No, Sam. Just…no," she says, walking out of my room and heading down the steps.

"Wait! Are you mad at me? Did I do something?" I ask from the top of the staircase.

She shrugs and puts her hand on the front door. "You want things that I don't. You want a girlfriend. I don't really… You've been so…" She shrugs but doesn't finish either thought. "I guess I'm just disappointed. I thought we could make this work without labels, but…" She shrugs again and closes the door behind her.

I go back to my room and stand in front of the window. I watch Marnie walk down my driveway, her heavy white coat wrapped around her. She adjusts the frog cap on her head before hunching over to avoid the wind and shoving her hands in her pockets.

She walks to the end of my driveway without ever looking back toward my window. My breath fogs up a small circle in front of my eyes. I wipe it away as Marnie turns left and starts walking up Ace's driveway. Only when she reaches his front porch does she turn and look back at my house.

13

TODAY
6:21 p.m.

My eyelids feel heavy, and I lean my head all the way back. My neck makes popping noises, but that doesn't relieve any of the pain crawling up my back. I try to breathe slowly and deeply, but my chest is hurting. I feel like a hundred bricks are sitting on my shoulders and my throat.

"You feeling tired, Sam?" Michael asks.

I just nod. My eyelids are so heavy.

"You look tired," he says.

I nod again.

"Are you ready to talk about Marnie yet?"

I turn my head to the side. I just want to go to sleep. Why won't they let me go to sleep? I flex my wrists and shift my weight.

"I love her," I say, my eyes closing.

"Does she love you?"

A hollow-sounding laugh forces its way out of my throat. "I think she used to," I say.

I let my eyes close, and I feel myself drifting. Back before it got complicated. Before she hated me. Before.

The bricks on my throat get lighter. My neck feels rubbery. It's dark and cool inside my head. I want to curl up and stay here. Where it doesn't hurt. Where nothing burns and nothing itches and nothing has weight.

"Sam? You awake?" Michael's voice pulls me back to the harsh light of the room.

I open my eyes enough to see Michael, his elbows leaning on his knees, the long-discarded tie in a puddle near his chair.

"She doesn't love you anymore? What happened?" he asks.

I turn my head toward the window again and fight against my dropping eyelids. What happened? What did happen? How do you just stop loving someone?

My voice comes out in a thin rasp. "Ace."

My eyes feel swollen now. Tiny slits that barely let in any light.

"So Marnie and Ace…Are they together?"

I shrug. My eyes are so heavy. The heaviness starts to spread down my face and pull down on my cheeks. My head dips backwards.

"Do you think we could talk about Ace, Sam? Would that

be okay?" Michael says. He moves his chair closer to me and pats my knee with one hand.

Ace.

"You've lived next door to Ace for most of your life, right? The Quinns moved in when you were pretty young?" Michael says softly.

I look toward the window again. The sun is starting to set. I can't see it, but I know it's setting because the light outside is turning pink. I blink a few times, and my eyes focus a little more.

"Yeah. Next door," I say.

"Were the two of you friends?" Michael asks.

Friends.

Mom says: "You dug in the sand together when you were five. I don't know what happened to the two of you."

Dad said: "You should try harder. He's a nice kid, a built-in buddy for you right next door."

Grandpa says: "You're always one step ahead of that guy," and then laughs.

"He hates me," I tell Michael.

"He hates you? Why do you say that?" he asks, writing something in his notebook.

"He hates me," I say again, the words clogging my throat.

"He hates you. Do you hate him?" Michael asks.

My eyes are too heavy to keep open anymore.

14

FEBRUARY
Three Months Before

Ace's living room is filled to the brim with the stuffed remains of furry, innocent woodland creatures. I've been in his house a few times, and I'll never get used to it. Ace stands near a gray squirrel, his latest taxidermied masterpiece, with a handful of his loyal followers.

"I was only about ten yards away, but I popped this little sucker right on the back of the head. Feel. Right there," he says to his buddies, touching the posed squirrel on the back of the head. "Got myself a red fox that trip too. Right over here." He points to a large shelf across the room. Turkeys, a handful of rabbits, and a raccoon all stare into the living room with their glass eyes. Most are posed on a wooden stand with an engraved placard attached. "ACE – AGE 11" reads the stuffed opossum next to me.

"Got this one a couple years ago," he says, pointing at a six-point buck head hanging on the wall. ACE – AGE 15, the placard reads. "Two hundred yards out. *Boom*," he says, mimicking holding a rifle and staring through a scope.

His followers look impressed.

I hurry out of the living room as quickly as I can manage.

In the hallway between the living room and the kitchen, there's a hog's head on the wall. Its mouth is open like it's screaming, and two curly horns poke out of its snout. ACE – AGE 17.

I run into Marnie in the kitchen. She's wearing Ace's Texas Longhorns sweatshirt and drinking something out of a red plastic cup.

"I'm celebrating!" she says, her cheeks bright pink and her eyes glassy.

"I think maybe you should slow down," I say, trying to take the plastic cup from her hand.

"You're not allowed to tell me what you think anymore," she says, her words slurring together just a little bit. A wide grin spreads across her face. "You and me…we're not together. We never really were," she says loudly, laughing.

"It doesn't mean I don't still care about you," I say. "As a friend."

"Well, *friend*, I'm a big girl. Go find someone else to mother," she says, her smile disappearing.

I watch her walk out of the kitchen and into the backyard. Ace comes through the kitchen and goes out shortly after Marnie does. He sneaks up behind her, pulling her into a bear hug. She gives him a drink out of her cup, and he slides his arm tighter around her waist.

I feel the tension start in my jaw and spread down to my shoulders. I'm crushing a cup in my hand when JC finds me.

"What up, superstar!" he says, his eyes shining.

"You too?" I say, turning to him.

"Me too, what?"

"How much have you had to drink?" I ask.

"Oh, come on. You know I don't do that. I'm riding a post-game high! Come on! You should be out there celebrating with us! We just won state, man! What are you doing in here alone?" JC puts his arm on my shoulder and tries to steer me toward the door.

I wiggle out of his grip. "Marnie's drunk," I say.

JC rolls his eyes. "No she's not. You can't spend the whole night worried about her, Sam. She'll be fine. And it's not up to you to worry about her anymore, anyway."

I look out the window and see Marnie and Ace curled up on a deck chair in the backyard. They are wrapped in a fuzzy blanket.

"I can't believe she's with him now," I say, watching them.

"You got to let that go," JC says. "Come on. I'll introduce you to some of Jeannie's sophomore friends. Nothing helps you get over a girl faster than another girl," he says, pulling me toward the door again.

I let myself be led.

* * *

The fire is warm, and it's one of the only things that's keeping me standing outside listening to this girl, Haley. Every other phrase out of her mouth is "like, ya know," and I want to put my hands over my ears. I've never been so bored in my life.

But I do have a bird's-eye view of Marnie and Ace in the deck chair from where I'm standing with Haley Like-Ya-Know. Ace has been running his hand up and down Marnie's jean-clad thigh for the past fifteen minutes. He buries his face in her hair.

Wildflowers. Spearmint.

My stomach drops.

"Like, do you have a date for the Winter Banquet yet?" Haley asks.

Marnie leans her head back on Ace's chest. He kisses her forehead and twists his finger around one of the curls she has swept behind her ear.

"Cuz I don't think I'm going this year," Haley says when I don't answer. "Last year it was, like, Loserville, ya know? Snooze City," she says, bumping into my arm.

Marnie pops up on her knees and kisses Ace's cheek before climbing out of the chair and walking back toward the sliding glass door.

"I'll be right back," I say to Haley.

I catch up to Marnie in the living room, just at the foot of the staircase.

"Where are you going?" I ask, louder than I intended.

"None of your business," she says with a smirk before continuing to climb the stairs and walk down the hall toward Ace's room.

The slider opens behind me.

Ace.

"She's drunk," I say to him when he closes the door.

Ace just stares at me. "Go to hell, Sam," he says weakly.

He climbs the stairs to his room and shuts the door behind him.

I glance at my watch. Ten forty-eight.

"Hey." JC appears beside me. "Haley's wondering where you went."

"I don't know, man. Haley's okay, but..." I say.

"Lighten up, North. She's cute, right? It's not like you have to marry her," JC says, trying to pull me back to the fire.

I glance at the stairs again. Ace's door is still closed. I look at my watch. Ten fifty-four.

"I gotta go to the bathroom," I say. "Tell Haley I'll be right back."

JC's eyebrows scrunch up, and he glances upstairs. "Bathroom?" he says.

"Yeah."

He lets out a big sigh. "You gotta let her go, Sam."

"I am! I have! Look! This is me, letting her go. Tell Haley I want to take her to the Winter Banquet. I'll be right back. Okay?" I say, trying to smile.

JC lets go of my arm and heads back outside.

I head right for the bathroom on the first floor. When I come out, the house is quiet. I glance through the slider and see everyone gathered by the fire. It's dark in the house.

I make my way through the living room, the dark, marbled eyes of Ace's stuffed trophies staring at me. I climb the stairs.

Outside his room, I hear music. A pale light is shining onto the floor from the crack under the door.

I glance at my watch. Eleven oh six.

They've been in there for eighteen minutes. Eighteen minutes. So many things could happen in eighteen minutes. Marnie could have passed out. Ace could be...

I can't think about that.

What if she passes out and gets sick and chokes?

It happens. They told us about it in health class in ninth grade.

I pace in front of the door.

I press my ear against it, but I don't hear anything but music.

It's been twenty-one minutes now.

Twenty-one minutes.

He could be...

What if she's not safe?

What if he's...

She had so much to drink.

I think she had so much to drink.

I need to get to her.

I need to stop him.

He'll kill me.

He would literally kill me.

Like the deer and the turkey, my head will be on a wooden stand with a placard underneath. ACE – AGE 17.

But what if she's...

What if he's hurting her, and she doesn't even know?

He'll kill me. Grab his shotgun, stare through the scope, and *boom*. Ten yards out.

She's not safe.

Twenty-seven minutes.

I have to stop him.

I hear shuffling behind Ace's door and quietly make my way back downstairs to the kitchen. I busy myself at the sink while Ace jogs down the steps, adjusting the waistband of his pants.

He goes outside and I follow.

"Yeah, right...Pictures or it didn't happen," one of Ace's cronies is saying when I get outside by the fire.

"I don't kiss and tell, gentlemen," Ace crows.

The crowd boos.

"But!" Ace says, his finger raised in the air. "Maybe there's a picture or two." He laughs.

The crowd cheers.

"Stud," one of the guys says to him.

Ace shakes his head and takes a drink. "Nah, seriously. She's upstairs asleep," he says, cheeks red.

"Well, which is it, man? You put her to sleep, or you *put* her to *sleep*," one of the guys on the football team says. Everyone laughs.

Nobody notices me sneak back into the house and climb the stairs. I open the door to Ace's room and see Marnie sound asleep, curled up in a dark-green comforter.

"Marn?" I whisper.

She doesn't answer.

I jiggle her shoulder a little bit. "You okay, Marnie?"

"Mmm...go away," she says, her voice faraway and sleepy. "Just need to lie here for a..."

I watch her breathe. Count how many times her chest rises and falls beneath the green comforter.

Seven...eight...nine...ten.

Ace's cell phone jingles on the nightstand.

Pictures or it didn't happen...

Maybe there's a picture or two, he said.

"Marn?" I whisper again.

The only answer is a soft snore.

A picture or two...

I grab Ace's phone and shove it in my pocket.

I run down the stairs and almost straight into JC.

"Where'd you disappear to? Haley's waiting outside for you," he says, trying to steer me back to the bonfire.

"I gotta go, man."

"What's going on with you?"

He's got pictures. Of her. With him. She's not safe.

"I just...I gotta go, JC," I say, shaking his hand from my arm and walking out the front door.

"Hey, wait! Sam!" JC is shouting, but I'm already gone. I take off through the front yard and jump the fence, my sneakers digging into the sandy ground between Ace's house and mine. I run all the way down my driveway and into the garage.

I pull the cell phone out of my pocket and put it on Dad's old workbench. I push the power button, and the screen lights up. A picture of Ace and Marnie together, kissing. I find Ace's video folder and touch the first thumbnail picture, dated last week. Immediately, a video starts to play. Marnie in a black tank top and Broadmeadow sweatpants, smiling on the screen. Marnie's giggle. Ace's voice. Marnie, in just a bra now, laughing and being silly for the camera. Some jumpy video of the sheets and then Marnie, on top of Ace. Her shy smile. She mouths "love you" to the camera. Ace's quiet laugh. The sick feeling washes from the top of my head all the way to my toes.

I pause the video with shaking fingers and shove the phone in my pocket. I can't watch anymore. I need to tell someone. I need to show them…Marnie. What was Ace going to do with this video? She's not safe with him.

"Mom!" I yell. "I need to talk to you," I say, heading toward the light in the kitchen. She'll know what to do. She'll know how to handle this.

"Mom, I need your help. I don't know what to—"

Mom and Grandpa are sitting at the kitchen table. Mom is crying into her hands, and Grandpa is rubbing her back.

"It may be time to go back, Jenny," Grandpa is saying.

Mom squeezes her fists into her eyes. She's nodding.

"It's okay, sweetheart," Grandpa says.

"Mom?" I say, coming into the kitchen. "What's going on?"

Grandpa looks at me. "Your mom is having a rough night," he says.

I sit down at the table. "Mom?"

"I think I need to go back to Morningside, Sam," she says.

Morningside. Where Mom learned yoga and breathing techniques and coping strategies and twelve steps and all the things she now teaches to others. Morningside. Where Mom decided to quit her job as a real estate agent. Morningside. Where she was prescribed a cocktail of chemicals that was supposed to keep her from having to go back.

"But I thought you and Cathy—"

"She needs more than Cathy can give her right now, Sam," Grandpa says, cutting me off.

"Mom?"

"I'm voluntarily going this time, Sam. I won't be gone as long...It'll be okay," she says, a smile touching her lips.

"But you got better...You were better," I say.

Mom wipes at her eyes with a tissue. "I'll be better again," she says.

The cell phone in my pocket buzzes. I don't look at it.

15

MARCH
Two Months Before

The next day, Mom loaded a suitcase full of yoga pants and T-shirts into a duffel bag and we drove her three hours up the coast to Morningside. She seemed stronger when we dropped her off, and I wondered for a minute why she decided that she needed this again.

"Why does she want to go back?" I asked on our way home.

Grandpa shrugged. "It's been getting worse for awhile, Sammy. It's not something that just goes away and never comes back."

"But Cathy, her therapist—"

Grandpa was shaking his head. "It's more than just Cathy can handle. I know she has tried to be strong around you, kiddo, but she's really been struggling. She knows herself,

Sam. I trust her. We can be strong for her. Men stand on their own two feet."

With that, he turned the vent on high and we didn't talk again all the way home.

The house is so quiet without Mom around. You never really give any thought to how much one person does in your life until that person is suddenly missing. Grandpa and I existed on a steady diet of cereal and frozen pizza for the first few days that Mom was gone. We've gotten into a routine now, though, one that doesn't rely so heavily on the microwave or foods with words like Krunch or Krispy on the box.

I keep Ace's cell phone in my sock drawer. I don't know what else to do with it. Sometimes I feel like I should have smashed it. I can't bring myself to do it, though. I disabled the Find My Phone app before I shoved it in the drawer, and for the first few days, it rang all the time. Mostly calls from Ace's home number. I'm sure he thought he lost it somewhere in the house. The calls stopped after awhile, and I'm sure he's gotten a new phone with a new number.

I take the phone out at night and look through the pictures in Ace's camera roll. Some are selfies of Ace and Marnie together. When I look at those, I put my thumb over Ace's face and pretend it's me standing next to Marnie. The most recent pictures are of Marnie in her cheer uniform. Some are close-ups of her face; others are from farther away. Some are silly, like she knew Ace was taking her picture and she'd make a face. Others are more serious, her eyes clouded and her expression still. I like those better. I look at those a lot.

I touch the text icon and a list of Ace's old text conversations pops up on the screen. I touch Marnie's name and scroll back a bit.

Marnie: Can't you just tell him?

Ace: No, he expects me to win everything. All the time.

Marnie: Well, that doesn't seem realistic.

Ace: It's not…but it would make me sound like a pussy if I said that.

Marnie: You're not a pussy, baby ☺

Ace: Ever since SAOTY, he's been on my ass. I don't know how I'm going to tell him I didn't get into Texas…

Marnie: I'm sorry, babe ☹

Ace: He's going to kill me. Somehow it'll be my fault because I let someone "beat me." Ugh…it's not going to be a good weekend. If you need me, I'll be running laps and doing push-ups in the garage all weekend, I'm sure.

I delete the conversation and turn the phone off.

* * *

I bring JC home from school one afternoon, and Mrs. Cushman waves me in from the front porch.

"How's my Sammy?" she asks, stretching her arm across my shoulders and squeezing.

"I'm okay, Mrs. Cushman," I mumble.

"I've got some casseroles in the freezer for you and your grandpa. Come in and get them. I've even printed the defrosting and reheating directions right on the packages," she says.

"Thank you, Mrs. C. Grandpa has a meeting tonight, but I'm sure we'll use them later this week," I say.

"Then you'd better come in and settle yourself right down. You're staying for dinner tonight. I insist," she says.

I look at the floor. "Thank you," I say.

JC and I go upstairs to his room.

"So have you called Haley yet?" he asks as soon as he shuts his bedroom door.

I just sigh.

"Come on, Sam. You told her like a month ago that you were going to take her to the Winter Banquet. It's next week! She's bought a dress and everything. She's really looking forward to it. It's all she and Jeannie talk about," he says, settling himself onto his bed with his calculus notebook open in his lap.

I sit backwards in his desk chair, my chin resting on the back. "I don't even know if I want to go," I say.

"What's going on with you? You're so out of it," he says, screwing up his face.

"With me? What's wrong with me? Oh gee, I don't know, JC. Let me think…" I say sarcastically.

"Hey, chill. I'm just saying you ought to—"

"I'm sick of being told what I 'ought' to do, *Dad*. God, get off my back. I don't really like Haley…She's like a little freaking baby. And while we're on the subject, I don't know why you're so into Jeannie," I say.

"Hey! Who asked you? What's your deal, Sam?" he asks, closing the notebook and sitting up at the edge of his bed.

"Just...whatever. Forget it," I say, pulling a paperback from the stack on JC's desk.

"Hey, I know you're stressed about your mom and everything, but you've been acting weird for a while now," he says.

"I said, forget it. I'm just in a bad mood."

I have Ace's cell phone. You wouldn't believe what I saw. I want to show you, but I'm afraid of what you'll think of me. What you'll say. He's going to hurt Marnie. Sometimes I hate him so much I feel like I could kill him. If it weren't for the promised escape of college in a few months, I probably would kill him.

"No, really, Sam. I've seen you in a bad mood before. This is...It's more than that. What's going on with you?"

I could kill him. I swear to God I could kill him.

"Have you talked to Marnie recently? Like in the past couple of weeks? Does she seem okay to you?" I ask.

JC shrugs. "She seems normal. I had lunch with her and Jeannie the other day when you had to retake that chemistry test. Why do you ask?"

I think Ace is convincing her to do things. I can't be sure. I don't know if she wanted it or not. But she was there and she looked completely out of it and I'm worried and I love her and if he hurt her, I swear to God. I want her to be okay. Holy fucking shit, I just want her to be okay.

"I'm worried about her," I say.

"I'm worried about you," he says.

I look right in JC's eyes. They dart back and forth over my face, and his eyebrows pull into the center of his forehead. He's leaning forward onto his knees and chewing on the end of his tongue like he does when he's nervous.

There's this black pit inside me, and sometimes when everything is quiet, I feel like it's going to open up and swallow me whole. Sometimes that scares me to death, and sometimes I think I could slip right down into that pit without a second thought. That I'd welcome it. The quiet. The peace. A place where I can't be a disappointment to anyone.

"I have—" I start to say.

"Boys! Dinner!" I hear Mrs. Cushman call from downstairs.

"One minute, Mom!" JC calls.

He turns to me. "You have what?"

JC is putting his books and notebooks into his backpack. Straightening up his bed and moving toward the door. "You have what?" he repeats.

"Nothing," I say. "It's nothing."

I open JC's bedroom door, and we head down to dinner.

To my surprise, Mr. Cushman has cleared off the table and a big spaghetti dinner is spread out.

"No TV trays?" I ask Mrs. Cushman with a smile.

"Not for my number one boys!" she says, pulling my head into her warm shoulder and kissing it.

We serve ourselves heaping helpings of spaghetti and bread

and salad, the clanging of spoons on plates the only noise. When we all have steaming plates in front of us, Mr. Cushman stands up at the head of the table and clinks his water glass with a fork.

"The mail was delivered earlier this afternoon," he says with a big flourish, producing a small stack of envelopes and handing them over to JC.

"Seriously? All of them came today?" JC says, his eyes shining.

"The last of them did. I've been holding on to them," he says sheepishly. "Open them up!"

My heart sinks a little bit. I look around the table. A linen tablecloth, drippy white candles in silver holders. Now I understand. College acceptance letters. Mr. and Mrs. Cushman want to make a big deal out of JC reading his letters tonight. That's why there are no TV trays. We're celebrating.

I think about my own mailbox. I may have a letter sitting in the box at the top of our driveway. Grandpa's in a meeting. Mom is...not home. The house is probably dark and cold. There will be no spaghetti dinner when I get home. No warm smells coming from the kitchen. No special dessert with my name spelled out in chocolate icing. The black pit opens.

"I got into UMass!" JC announces, and Mr. and Mrs. Cushman produce noisemaker horns from their laps.

Toot, toot! They blow into the horns and clap.

I sit down on the curb and stare at the Oceanside envelope. I can't make myself open it.

"What the hell are you doing, Samantha?" Ace appears at the end of his driveway, shirtless and bathed in yellow streetlight. He's holding a piece of paper in his hand.

I stand up from the curb and brush the sand from my pants. I'm clawing my way out of that pit.

"What the fuck do you care?" I ask, spitting on the ground a few inches from Ace's bare feet.

He cocks his head to the side and smiles with great big crocodile teeth. "I don't, asshole."

He walks slowly toward me and snatches the envelope from my hands. "Oceanside, huh? Let's have a look-see, faggot," he says, ripping it open.

I try to grab it from him. He just jerks his hand back and laughs. "Scholar-athlete, my ass," he says.

"Look at that. You're in," he says, throwing my letter from Oceanside onto the ground.

I stand up as tall as I can and approach Ace. I get right up in his face, and he doesn't back down. "I'll finally be rid of you," I say quietly. I'm not afraid. I'm not frozen. I reach the top of the pit, and I'm pulling myself onto solid ground and—

"Oh, that's where you're wrong, dear Samantha," he says. He puts the piece of paper from his hand right onto my chest. "Read it and weep, asshole. You'll never be rid of me. I'll always be right there. Right behind you. Right in your rearview mirror. Oh no, Samantha. You'll never be rid of me," he whispers right in my ear.

He lets his letter drop onto the ground and walks back toward his driveway.

"Fuck you!" I yell toward him.

I start to shake from my bones outward. Ace turns on his heel and slowly saunters back into the middle of the street. "What did you say to me?" he whispers when he finally reaches me.

"I said, fuck you." Goose bumps pop up on my arms and I am sick to my stomach.

Ace leans toward me and puts his mouth right up next to my ear. "You might want to watch how you talk to me, QB2," he whispers, his breath tickling the inside of my ear. "I'm not twelve years old anymore," he says.

He turns on his heel and walks into his house. I sit down in the middle of the street, my breath ragged and my skin raw and burning. I pick up both letters from Oceanside.

> Dear Dean Quinn Jr.,
> We are pleased to offer you a scholarship for the coming school year. There was a staggering number of applicants this year, and you should be very proud that you have been selected...

> Dear Samuel North,
> We are pleased to offer you a scholarship for

the coming school year. There was a staggering
number of applicants this year, and you should
be very proud that you have been selected...

It's not going to stop. It's never going to stop.

16

APRIL
One Month Before

JC and I haven't spoken since I stormed out of his house a few weeks ago. I know I should apologize, but I don't even know what I would be apologizing for. I catch him looking at me during lunch. I sit alone by the door to the courtyard. Sometimes I eat.

Mostly I don't.

Marnie is walking into school just a few steps ahead of me. I could reach out and touch her back if I stretched far enough.

"Marn," I say.

She turns around with a two-dimpled smile, but it fades when she sees that it's me that called her.

"Hey," I say.

"What is it, Sam?" she asks, examining her pinkie nail.

"Can we talk later? Just talk. I just...uh...I just need your help with something," I say.

Marnie pinches her lips together and glances at her watch.

"Can you just meet me in the library at lunch today? Please? I promise it won't take long," I say.

She takes a deep breath in through her nose. "Yeah. Sure," she says and turns on her heel and walks away quickly.

I let out a long breath.

A few hours later, I drop my pass in the librarian's bucket and make my way to the back corner of the room. A big couch sits in front of a bank of windows, overlooking Broad Creek. The couch might be my favorite place in the whole school. Luckily, it is largely unused because Mrs. Otwell, the school librarian, isn't too keen on letting more than one student use it at a time. She says that sitting on couches makes everyone think they're at a party—and this is a library. Sometimes I think she'd drop the couch in the Dumpster if she could lift it on her own. Since I am alone, she says nothing as I make my way back there and pull out my chemistry notebook.

A few minutes later, Marnie appears at the couch.

"You came," I say.

"Of course I did. I don't hate you, Sam," she says, rolling her eyes.

I push my notebook into my backpack and move over on the couch and pat the cushion for Marnie to sit down. She glances toward Mrs. Otwell's desk at the front of the room.

She's not there, so Marnie settles herself on the very edge of the cushion.

"What did you want to talk to me about?"

"How have you been?"

"Fiiiiiine…" she says.

"Good. That's good."

"Look, Sam. JC told me what happened at his house the other night. He's really worried about you," she says, pulling a nail file out of her purse. "Why aren't you talking to him?"

I watch her and see the old Marnie. The Marnie that loved me. Twelve-year-old Marnie that brought me peanut butter and jelly sandwiches when my dad died. The Marnie that lay on my bed eating Cheez-Its and drinking grape soda and laughing at YouTube videos with me. The Marnie that liked to ride in my truck with both windows open and the bass on my radio pounding. The Marnie that tucked notes into my locker and threw pebbles at my window at night. I miss her so much it hurts.

I pull my backpack onto my lap and shrug. "I don't really want to talk about that," I say.

"Whatever. JC's been your best friend forever, though, Sam. He's really hurt," she says.

I shrug again. This isn't how I pictured this conversation.

"Listen, I need to ask you something," I say. I dig my hand into my hoodie pocket and squeeze my hand around Ace's cell phone.

"Go for it," she says, blowing on her fingernails.

"Are you...Ace and you...Have you..."

"Spit it out, Sam."

I hesitate. I have to know. I have to know if he was... "Are you sleeping with Ace?"

She drops the nail file on the couch, and her jaw drops along with it. "Are you kidding me? That's none of your business," she says, throwing her backpack over her shoulder and standing up from the couch. "Seriously? That's why you called me here? I swear to God, Sam—"

"No! It's not like that! I just...I'm so worried about you, Marn," I say.

"Quit it! Quit acting like this, Sam! This jealousy...It's ridiculous," she says, her voice getting louder.

"It's not jealousy. Ever since the party after state, I just... Are you safe?"

"Safe? What are you even talking about?" she says. "JC was right. You have totally lost your mind. We're not together anymore, Sam," she says, wagging her index finger back and forth between the two of us. "What am I saying? We never really were together, and what I do with my boyfriend is none of your business."

With that, she stomps out of the library and leaves me alone on the couch.

I put my head back and cover my eyes with my forearm.

"What are you doing, North?" I hear. I feel someone sit down on the couch next to me.

I uncover my eyes, and Ace is sitting next to me. Close. Too close. His face is just a few inches from mine. I pull my shoulders back into the couch as far as I can.

"Talking to my girlfriend in the library?" he says.

"It's not like that," I say, swallowing hard.

"Do I make you nervous, Sam?"

I don't answer. My fingers are squeezed around the seam on the arm of the couch. I can feel my pulse pounding on the side of my throat.

"I hope I make you nervous," he says. "Maybe I'll make you so nervous that you'll have to go live with your mommy upstate. Is that what you'd like? I'm sure that loony bin has some nice padded walls for you and your crazy mommy to bang your heads on."

"Shut up," I say, my voice cracking.

Ace laughs. "You scared, little buddy? Aww...Did I scare you the other night? Is that why you needed to talk to Marnie? Think she's going to protect you?"

I'm only inhaling as Ace inches closer and closer to my face. His voice is getting quieter.

"I will always be right here, Sam. Marnie's not going to protect your sorry ass." He is so close that his breath tickles my nose.

My back presses into the corner of the couch, and all the muscles in my thighs are tight, ready to jump and run.

Ace puts the tip of his nose right on my nose.

"Boo, motherfucker," he whispers. He hops up from the couch and is gone.

* * *

It's three a.m., and my eyes are wide open. The moon is so bright it lights up my entire bedroom. I pull on my hoodie and shove my hand into the pocket. The phone is still safely tucked inside. I turn it on and flip through a couple of pictures. Marnie making a duck face in Ace's Jeep. A profile shot of Marnie reading, her hair piled on top of her head, a few stray curls sweeping across her cheek. Marnie smiling: one dimple. I scroll back to the picture of Marnie reading and trace the curl on her cheek.

I quietly open my bedroom door.

Sneaking out of my house is ridiculously easy now that Mom is gone. Grandpa sleeps like a rock. I don't even have to go out the window and shimmy down the tree anymore. I can just open the front door and walk out. I trudge along the sandy driveway and into the cul-de-sac. There are no lights on at Ace's house, and his Jeep is parked crookedly in the driveway.

I walk quickly through the neighborhood, the street lamps glowing. I don't even have to think to get where I'm going. Left turn, left turn, right turn. Third house on the left.

Marnie's bedroom is in the back of the house. I walk slower as I approach. None of the houses on her street have their porch lights on, and I only have to avoid the pools of streetlight. I walk quietly through the dewy grass, my shoes sinking slightly into the wet ground. I crouch down and approach Marnie's window slowly.

My breath fogs her window slightly, and I use my hoodie sleeve to wipe away the mist. The light from her alarm clock casts a blue glow across her face and chest. I watch her breathe. Count the number of times her chest rises and falls. Her curls fall across her forehead and onto her pillowcase.

She's safe. My hand curls around the phone in my pocket. She's safe for now.

* * *

"I'm leaving at noon to pick up your mom, Sam," Grandpa tells me ten days later at breakfast.

"So you won't be at school?" I ask.

Grandpa shakes his head. I want to ask him more, but he puts the morning paper up between us and sips his coffee slowly.

"Grandpa?" I say quietly.

"What is it?" he says without moving the paper.

"Do you think she's ready? To come home?"

He folds the paper, exhaling slowly through his nose the whole time. He looks right at me and folds his hands in front of him.

"I think we'll make the best of it, Sammy," he says. "You know I've visited a time or two. She's definitely better than she was in February. We'll be strong for her. Summer is coming.

- 177 -

I'll be home. You'll be around more. We'll be okay," he says, offering me a very small smile.

"Do you want me to come with you this afternoon?" I offer. Three hours in the car on the way to the hospital. That's a lot of space for talking. *Please say yes, Grandpa. Please say you want my company. Please ask me to come with you.*

"Nah," he says, picking up the newspaper again. "You get yourself to school. I got this."

I grit my teeth. Grandpa doesn't lower the paper. If he lowers the paper, I'll tell him. I'll tell him what this feels like. I'll tell him I need him. If he lowers the paper again, I'll say it. *I'm slipping into a hole, Grandpa. I'm drowning.*

"You'd better skedaddle, Sammy. Don't you have a test today?" he says, turning the page of the newspaper, but not looking at me.

The tension in my jaw travels down my neck and into my chest where it rests like a concrete block. I grab my backpack from the living room and head out to my truck. I pull the zipper on my black hoodie all the way up to my chin and yank the hood over my head. I put my hands in my pocket and feel Ace's cell phone. I leave it in there and climb into the truck. The April sun beats through my window, but I barely feel it at all.

I sit in my truck in the back corner of the senior parking lot until the warning bell rings. Ace and Marnie arrive together. Marnie looks right at me when she hops out of the passenger seat of Ace's Jeep. She doesn't smile with one dimple or two.

* * *

Last period of the day is chemistry lab with Dr. Gunther. And Marnie. We used to be lab partners, but Marnie asked to switch last semester after the Great Breakup. Now my lab partner is a girl who wears black every day and smells like cookies. That probably sounds like a dream to some guys: a girl who smells like cookies. But this girl smells like the cookies your grandma offers you from the blue tin after Christmas. Not like fresh-baked chocolate-chip goodness or anything. There's a huge difference.

I drag my feet getting to class, knowing we're doing some experiment today. Which means I'll actually have to work. I can't just sit there and pretend to take notes, my closed eyes hidden behind my hoodie.

The first thing I notice when I enter the room is that the smelly cookie girl is absent today. So is Marnie's lab partner.

"North and Keaton, you're together today," Dr. Gunther says when the bell rings.

"Oh, come on, Dr. Gunther," Marnie starts to protest.

Dr. Gunther adjusts his glasses with his left thumb knuckle like he always does. "I don't want to hear it, Ms. Keaton. You and North are both without lab partners today, and you absolutely need a partner for today's lab. You're together. Now move your things to Mr. North's table, please," he says, turning toward the whiteboard and uncapping a dry-erase marker.

Marnie makes as much noise as she can pulling out her lab stool and grabbing the bucket of supplies from underneath the table. She steps heavily across the room and sits down with a loud sigh at the empty stool at my lab table.

The whole room watches her, including Dr. Gunther. "Are you quite finished?" he says when she finally settles in and lets out an aggravated hissing noise.

"Yes, sir," she mumbles.

"Sorry," I say to her as Dr. Gunther turns to write the lab steps on the whiteboard.

"Sorry I'm stuck with you? Or sorry you're stuck with me?" she says.

I don't answer.

Dr. Gunther writes "Catalase Kinetics" and starts talking in chemistry terms I barely understand. I used to have an A in chemistry.

"…measure the effects of changes in temperature…"

"Are you going to stop following me, Sam?"

I don't answer.

"Seriously. It's getting creepy."

I don't answer, but write down the lab steps in my notebook. I lean my chin on my hand and keep my eyes down. Old me bubbles to the surface, and the only thing keeping him inside is my hand on my cheek. I flex my fingers and squeeze the skin on my face to keep him in.

He touched you. I watched. He would have put that shit on the

Internet if I hadn't stolen his phone. *You should be thanking me, and you don't even know it.*

"Are you going to talk to me, or are you just going to sit there and pretend you can't hear me?"

I love you. I love you I love you I love you and I can't stop thinking about you and why did you leave me and why are you with Ace now and how come it's okay for him to treat you like that and why do you hate me why why why.

I say nothing. Squeeze my fingers against my cheek so tightly that my wrist starts to shake. I'm sweating in my hoodie, but I don't take it off. It swallows the old me whole. It keeps him inside. It keeps the words in.

That Fourth of July at the beach, the first night she kissed me, is so close to the surface. I know that if I don't keep my hoodie wrapped tight around me, if I don't keep my fingers against my cheek, it will all spill out, all over this lab table. All the things I see when I look at her. Kindergarten Marnie scoring a basket, long braids bouncing down her back. Middle school Marnie at my father's wake, making a heart with her hands. Marnie and me, watching the sunset from the lifeguard chair. Marnie and me, sneaking out and going down to the beach at three in the morning. Marnie, pressed against my chest behind the field house. Marnie, in the front seat of my truck before school every morning. Marnie, with me.

Marnie sighs that big dramatic sigh again, air rushing from her mouth and across the desk hard enough to rustle the pages in my notebook. "I don't know what happened to you, Sam," she says, getting up from the table to gather the needed chemicals from the supply closet.

She stands in line at the closet, hand on her hip.

"You happened," I say to my notebook.

* * *

There are glimpses of the old me that cared. Sometimes I can see the deep-blue flame of his thoughts licking at the corners of my eyes. When I look at her, he's there. Or when I'm just waking up and that heavy blanket of shit hasn't quite settled around me yet. He's there. His bright eyes and quick smile haunt me from inside my own head. Sometimes he pounds inside my brain. It hurts and it burns and it sucks. I want him to go away.

And yet.

Sometimes he's close. So close that I wonder if he'll fight his way to the surface. If his will be the voice I hear if I try to talk. If his clothes will be what I put on in the morning. If everyone will see him.

And other days, it's like he never existed at all.

Today is not one of those days.

I wake up with his thoughts in my head.

Marnie. Today is her birthday. Did I buy her a card? Should I stop to get a bunch of flowers from the gas station before I pick her up? Did I call ahead and make reservations at her favorite place for dinner?

When I swing my legs onto the floor, he's gone. For now.

He'll be back, shining his light around in my head, looking for a way out. I won't be able to stop it, as much as I wish I could. When that old me is in there, I can feel him scratching.

I drive by her house when I leave the neighborhood. Left turn, left turn, right turn, third house on the left. There are two shiny helium balloons on the mailbox: one in the shape of the number one, and one in the shape of the number eight. Ace's car is in her driveway. I wonder if he is the one who put the balloons there. I drive slowly by, glancing down the driveway and wondering if I'll see her if I drive slowly enough. I know that's the old me, pushing on my forehead from the inside.

I drive away when I see the front door open. It may not even have been them. It might have been Marnie's mom, ready for work with her black briefcase and *clicky-clacky* shoes. I know it wasn't her dad. His SUV wasn't in the driveway. I glance at my watch. Mr. Keaton probably left at least two hours ago. That was something old me knew.

I end up at the gas station, pulled into a parking space in the corner near the vacuum that doesn't work and the air pump that takes two dollars in quarters to operate. I know they will come here next. I've been watching. Ace will buy a can of Red Bull and sometimes a bag of Doritos. Marnie, a pack of sugarless gum. Spearmint. Always spearmint. From my parking spot, I will see them.

I think about going in and buying the flowers anyway. Maybe putting them in her locker. Maybe walking up to her in this gas-station parking lot, right in front of Ace, and giving them to her. That old me just won't go away, no matter how many times I've tried to get rid of him.

Ace comes out of the store first, holding the door open for Marnie. Neither one of them even looks toward me.

I feel invisible.

Powerful.

Marnie thanks him for holding the door with a kiss on his cheek. He smiles and she laughs and they look like a commercial for mouthwash. Or soap. Something wholesome.

I shut my eyes tight, squeezing the lids together until I see colored spots. When I open them again, Ace's Jeep is leaving the parking lot, turning right and heading toward Broadmeadow. When the swimming dots clear from my eyes, I leave the gas station too.

* * *

If I could skip lunch all together, I would. If there were somewhere to hide, somewhere to go where I could be invisible, I'd do it. Old me loved having lunch in the cafeteria. The place to see and be seen. Old me was all about being seen.

Right now I just want to blend into the wall.

I stand in the line and grab a basket of soggy fries and a package of Swiss Rolls. Scanning the room for an empty chair near the wall, I see Marnie at a spot right in the middle of the cafeteria. Four or five other girls surround her, but she's definitely the one holding court. Her eyes dance and her curls bounce while she tells a story. Only one dimple. A real smile. Old me pushes on my forehead again. Desperate to join her table. Listen to her stories. Laugh along with her.

I find an empty blue plastic chair at JC's table. I know he won't mind if I sit with him. I also know he won't mind if I don't talk. He won't ask any questions. He might pretend that I'm not even there.

"What up, Sammy? Long time, no see," JC says, putting his hand up for a high five when I approach his table of friends.

"Hey." I don't return the high five.

I sit sideways in the chair, my back against the wall, and pull my hoodie over my head again. I smother the fries in ketchup and eat them with my fingers. Ketchup goes everywhere.

JC and the other guys at the table continue to talk about some concert they're all going to this weekend at the university. The biggest debate seems to be whether to try and score a case of beer before they leave or wait until they get to the campus.

"If we get stopped for speeding and there's a case in my trunk, we're screwed," one guy with a nose piercing says.

"They don't look in your trunk if they pull you over for speeding, douche canoe," the zittiest guy says.

"Kaplan's right, Adam. We're not going to get pulled over either. Plus we know we can score a case at Kaplan's uncle's place before we leave. If we wait, we might have a hard time...procuring the provisions." JC says that last part under his breath.

The zitty guy, Kaplan, nods.

I snort.

JC shoots me a look. "Problem?" he asks.

"Nope. Just listening. Don't mind me. Pretend I'm not even here," I say, dragging a floppy fry through the ketchup soup in the basket.

Kaplan and Adam get up to throw their trash away. It's just JC and me at the table now. "Since when do you drink, JC?" I ask.

"Since when do you care, Sam?" he shoots back.

"Touché. I was just sayin'."

"Well, I'm just sayin' too. Why are you sitting here? You don't even talk to me anymore. What do you care what I do on the weekends? You're acting like an ass," JC says.

I just shrug.

Old me would have apologized. Correction. Old me never would have stopped hanging out with JC in the first place. And now old me is punching and kicking. *Apologize. Apologize. Apologize. JC would understand. Tell him. Tell him. Tell him you're drowning.*

"Whatever. I'm not going to waste my time anymore. You talk to me or don't talk to me. I don't give a shit," JC says, taking a sip of milk all defiant-like. Old me can feel the hurt radiating off JC's skin. *Stop him. Tell him. He will help you. He will see.*

I pull my hoodie strings tighter and put my feet up in the chair next to me. Shrug.

Kaplan and Adam come back, each with an ice cream sandwich. "Bitch alert, twelve o'clock," Kaplan says, motioning behind him with his head.

Marnie is marching toward this table. And truly, marching is the only way I can describe it. Her shoulders are back, and her mouth is set in a defiant sneer. She's staring right at me.

I sit up and put my feet flat on the floor.

She's coming this way.

Take your hood off your head.

She's coming right for you.

Wipe the ketchup off your lip.

She's coming. Right for you.

"Hey," she says when she reaches the table.

It's not a "Hey, how are you" kind of hey. It's more like a "You're a damn jerk, and I'm about to tell you just how jerky you are" kind of hey.

"Hey," I say back.

Don't look at her eyes. Just don't look at her eyes. You'll stop listening if you look at her eyes. Don't do it, Sam.

"Look at me," she says.

Damn it all.

My eyes slide up and meet her icy stare.

"Why were you at the gas station this morning?" she asks.

JC jerks his head toward me, his eyes wide.

"I wasn't..." I start to lie.

"Oh, come on, Sam. I saw your truck. I know that truck.

Why are you doing this? Why are you following me?" she asks, folding her arms across her chest and jutting out her hip.

"I'm not. I'm allowed to get gas, aren't I?"

"You're a stalker, Sam North. A stalker! Stay away from me! And stay away from Ace!" She is shouting now, and the whole cafeteria has their eyes on me.

Old me would have cared.

Old me would have been mortified.

Run after Marnie and apologized.

I walk to the trash can, my hoodie pulled over my eyes and dump my still-full tray of fries. I shove the Swiss Rolls into my pocket and walk outside to the courtyard.

Through the window, I see her talking to JC. His eyebrows have crawled all the way up to his hairline. Her curls are flying as she bobs her head all around. No dimples anymore. She keeps pointing through the window and throwing her hips all over the place. I don't know that I've ever seen her that pissed.

Stalker.

That's what she called me.

I want her to be safe. I'm just watching to make sure she's safe.

I wish I could say that her opinion of me doesn't matter.

17

TODAY
7:57 p.m.

The clock on the wall is loud. When Michael isn't talking, I can hear the *tick, tick, tick, tick, tick* like it's a brass band right in my head. I put my hands up to my ears and squeeze. Everything is noise.

"You okay, Sam?" Michael asks. Purple smudges are beginning to appear under his eyes. He has unbuttoned the top few buttons of his dress shirt and untucked it.

"I'm tired. I just want to close my eyes for a little bit," I say, my head lolling to the side. My voice sounds froggy, and my throat burns from the effort of forming a sentence.

"You can sleep soon, Sam. I promise. There are a few more things I need to ask you, okay?" Michael says.

I run my forearm across my eyes, and pain shoots through

"I tried to tell someone, Michael," I say quietly.

Michael says nothing, only pulls his chair closer to me. My throat closes up as he puts his hand on my shoulder.

"I tried to tell them..." I say, the lump in my throat dissolving. Tears drip onto my cheeks, and I don't wipe them away.

"I know you did, Sam," he says. He puts his notebook and pen on the floor and takes my right hand in both of his. "I know."

I let Michael hold my hand, and I close my eyes. The tears come through, and I don't try to stop them.

"I wanted someone to hear me."

18

MAY
One Day Before

I pull my black hoodie on even though it's going to be close to eighty degrees today. I reach into the right pocket and squeeze my hand around Ace's cell phone. It's with me every day. As long as I have it, she will be safe.

I glance at my alarm clock. Fifteen minutes before I have to leave for school. I head downstairs, knowing I'll find Mom on the sunporch, meditating. Since she came home from Morningside, she wakes up before the sun rises and spends the early part of the morning in deep meditation. I don't know what she's thinking about for that long, but she seems at peace.

I find Mom, but she's shoving papers into her laptop bag. Her sunglasses are on her head, and her car keys are in her hand.

"Where are you going?" I say, my stomach full of butterflies.

She turns and gives me a big smile. "Work!"

"You're going to work? Are you—"

"I'm fine," she says, her eyebrows raised and her voice stern.

"Yeah, but maybe you should give it another—"

Her lips purse and she blinks slowly. "You should probably leave for school, Sam. You don't want to be late."

I watch her check and recheck her bag. I want to tell her. *I'm sinking, Mom. I'm in so deep and I can't move.*

Mom, help.

I squeeze the cell phone in my hoodie pocket. *Help.*

"Get going, pokey!" She laughs, pushing me out the door and getting into her Volkswagen. "I'll see you tonight, sweetheart," she says, backing out of the driveway.

"But are you sure—"

She just waves her hand at me dismissively. I stand in the driveway and watch her drive all the way down the street to the curve. Her taillights disappear, but still I watch.

I sit down in my truck, but I don't know what to do next. My fingers clutch the steering wheel, and all I feel is empty. Forgotten. Used up. I don't even know if I have the strength to turn the key in the ignition. I close my eyes.

A fist bangs on my window.

Ace.

I roll down the window.

"Hi," he says, not smiling.

I nod my head, but say nothing. I grip the steering wheel tighter, my knuckles turning pink, then white, then purple.

"Are they warming up your rubber room upstate, Samantha?" he asks.

I don't even have the energy to reply.

He glances toward his house and then crouches down and puts his face through my window.

"I'm watching you. You're slipping, Samantha. You're not the Golden Boy everyone thinks you are, are you? You know what that means? No more second best for Ace Quinn. I win. I. Win."

I am outside my truck, and my hands are around Ace's thick neck before I even realize what I'm doing. Ace grabs my wrists and twists them away from his neck.

"Are you sure you want to do that again, Sam? Remember what happened when we were twelve. You hit me first. That was your first mistake," he says, his voice quiet and even.

"You came at me with a knife, asshole."

"I popped your basketball, you pussy. I didn't come at you with a knife." He laughs again.

"Stay away from me, you stupid fuck." I say, not moving away from him.

"That's rich, Samantha. Stay away from you? I'm going to be right here, right over your shoulder every time you turn around. Every time you think you're alone, I'll be there. Every time you think you're rid of me, I'll be right there. Waiting.

You need to be kept in your place," he says.

He backs away from me toward his house. His eyes never leave my face.

I am frozen to my driveway.

"I will always be bigger. I will always be faster and better than you, North. If you hit me first, I will hit back stronger and harder than you ever could. You should have figured that out when we were twelve. I will always win," he says, opening the door to his Jeep and climbing in.

He peels out of the driveway and heads down the street.

I don't move from my spot in the driveway until his tail-lights disappear.

* * *

Mr. Patton's office is painted a shade of green that can only be described as baby food peas, as are all the guidance counselors' offices.

"Sam, have a seat, kiddo," he says when I arrive at his door.

I hate that he calls me "kiddo."

He has a file folder opened in front of him. "So where are we?" he asks.

"Where are we?" *WE are nowhere, asshole.*

"College applications. Have you received your acceptance letters yet? Let's see where we've applied..." He flips through the papers inside the folders. "Just Oceanside, kiddo?" Mr. Patton asks, lowering his glasses and letting them hang around his neck like a grandma.

"It's the only place I want to go," I say, leaning back in my chair.

"Have you heard from them yet?"

I pull on my hoodie string and feel it creep tighter around my neck. "They offered me a scholarship to play basketball," I answer quietly.

"That's wonderful! I trust you accepted?" Mr. Patton sits forward in his chair, a genuine smile on his face.

I bite my lip to keep the old me from bubbling through. I haven't even picked up a basketball since February. I nod and look down at a stain on the leg of my jeans.

"That's really good news, Sam. Something to be proud of," Mr. Patton says. "So tell me, kiddo, how are things? Everything going well at home?"

I stare at the stain a little longer. Not quite round, more of an oval shape. *Tell him. Tell him you're drowning.*

"Your mom doing well?" he asks, lowering his glasses again.

I nod. My lips won't part. I can't look him in the eye.

"That's wonderful news, wonderful news. Well, sounds like you're all in order. It's good talking with you," Mr. Patton says, shuffling a few papers on his desk and looking up at the clock on the wall.

You're not twelve years old anymore, Sam.

"There's something I kind of want to talk to someone about," I say, picking at the stain on my jeans.

Mr. Patton looks at his watch out of the corner of his eye and pushes his chair back a bit. "Do you want to make another appointment?" he asks, pulling a pen from the cup on the desk and swiftly turning pages in his appointment book.

"No...I-I thought we could just talk about it now," I say, sitting up in the chair a little straighter. *I'm drowning. I'm drowning. I'm going to hurt him, or he's going to hurt me. The cycle is never going to end, and I can't I can't I can't...*

A face appears in the rectangular glass window in Mr. Patton's door. Mr. Patton stands up and puts his finger up to the glass. "One minute," he mouths through the window to Ace.

Ace doesn't leave. He continues to stand with his face in the window.

Mr. Patton doesn't sit back down, only stands with his back to the door. "I only have another minute or two until my next appointment, Sam. Are you sure you don't want to come back tomorrow? I can schedule as much time as you need," he says, glancing at his watch again.

"I'm...I'm just..." *drowning. Help me. Make it stop. Throw me a rope. Get me out of this.*

Mr. Patton rocks back and forth on his heels and folds his hands across his chest. His jaw flexes, and he looks at his watch again.

"I'm really happy about my scholarship to Oceanside," I say, throwing my backpack over my shoulder and grabbing for the door handle all in one motion. I walk as fast as I can past Ace and into the hallway before I take a full breath.

I lean against the wall, and my legs melt underneath me. I slide down until I'm sitting on the floor, my backpack scrunched up behind me like a pillow. When I do take a long breath, it's ragged and thick. My throat feels like it's closing, and my ears fill with the sound of rushing blood. I cover them with my palms, but nothing makes it stop.

Grandpa.

I stand up and run through the hallways, past the gym to Grandpa's office. He'll help me. He'll stop the drowning. He'll pull me out of this.

He'll know how to make it stop.

I reach for the door handle. Locked. The sign on the door says "Administrative meeting. Be back at 2." I eye the mailbox attached to the wall outside Grandpa's office. Grandpa put it up so that students would stop trying to shove papers and forms under the door. I sit down on the floor again and pull a notebook from my backpack.

Dear Grandpa,

No. No, I can't start like that.

There is something I need to talk to you about.

No, that's not right either.

How do I tell him? Men are supposed to stand on their own two feet. Men don't ask for help. Men take care of things on their own. That's what he always says.

How do I tell him that the pain in my chest is too much and I can't get away? I'm never going to be able to get away from it. Ace will follow me to college, and he'll always be there. Behind me. Waiting for me. And when I'm alone…when Grandpa isn't there anymore…The gloves are off. I'm on my own. There's no one left. Marnie doesn't care and JC doesn't understand and Dad is gone and Mom can barely take care of herself. I'm not safe. I'm not safe not safe not safe.

I can end this. I can make it all go away with just one squeeze of my index finger. Gone. Gone. Gone. *I won't be a disappointment.*

"I will not be a disappointment," I write on a corner of the paper. Ripping it from the notebook, I shove it in the mailbox and head out the gym doors to my truck. I know what I have to do.

19

MAY
Thirteen Hours Before

The gun lives in a safe in the linen closet in the laundry room. I tiptoe down the stairs, concocting a story in my head in case Mom or Grandpa wakes up. I need a towel. I have to change the sheets on my bed. I thought I heard a noise. With a flashlight trained on the back wall of the closet, I spin the combination lock on the safe.

24 right.

11 left.

47 right

Click.

Picking the gun up, I feel its weight in my hand. The rubber grip on the handle is slightly sticky against my palm. I pop open the chamber and pull the box of bullets from under a towel on the top shelf of the linen closet. I slide six bullets into the chamber, touching the golden ends with my index finger.

The first time Grandpa Carl took me to the rifle range, he showed me how to load the bullets into the cylinder of the .38 special.

"Look, Sammy, pointy edge toward the front. The flat side will sit nice and snug in the opening, there. See?" He handed me two bullets and let me drop them into the last two open slots in the cylinder.

Chink. Chink. I still remember the distinct sound of the bullets sliding in. Grandpa snapped the revolver shut then and put the giant green earmuffs over my ears. He aimed at the man-shaped target at the end of the range and shot all six bullets straight through the chest area of the man.

"Whoa, Gramps! If that was a real man..." I said, in awe.

"If that was a real man, he wouldn't be walking out of here," Grandpa said, laughing. "But listen...you should never need more than one bullet, Sammy. You should be able to do everything you need to do with just one bullet. When you know how to use it correctly, the gun will keep you safe, Sam."

I snap the revolver closed again and turn the gun over in my hand a few times.

Put it in your pocket. Just put it in your pocket.

I close the safe, spin the lock, and silently leave the laundry room with the gun in my front pocket.

I climb the stairs to my room and close the door behind me.

My backpack lies at the foot of the bed. I pull out the dirty PE clothes, a few crumpled class notes, and a half-eaten granola bar from the bottom of the bag. I unzip and re-zip every pocket on the bag before pulling the gun out of my pocket and laying it on the bed.

I grab the dirty Broadmeadow PE shirt and wrap the gun inside it before sliding it back into the front pouch of the backpack.

I undress and put on pajama pants and slide under the covers in my bed, my backpack within reach right next to me on the bed. I reach over to the window and slide the blinds up just enough to see his garage.

The door is open, and the lights are on. I can see Mr. Quinn standing near the weight bench with his arms folded across his chest, and Ace doing crunches nearby. I watch for a few minutes. Tomorrow.

I lie down and can only see his driveway now. The shiny black Jeep sits at an angle, the streetlight gleaming right down on the hood. I keep the blinds up.

Close my eyes. I can see it. It might still be dark in the morning before school, but with that streetlight shining right onto the Jeep, I'll have no problem.

Pop. Between the eyes.

Pop. In the throat.

PopPopPopPop. Right through the chest of the man-shaped target.

20

TODAY
8:19 p.m.

I don't want to open my eyes. The light burns and makes me forget who I am. In the dark behind my eyelids, I think I can remember that boy.

I hear Michael's pen scratching across his paper, so I know he's still in the room with me. "Is it easier for you to keep your eyes closed?" he asks quietly.

I nod.

"Can you tell me about this morning? Did you drive yourself to school? Did you talk to anyone?" Michael's voice speaks directly to that boy that I remember.

This morning.

This morning I thought about Marnie.

Every morning I think about Marnie.

Before I open my eyes and the light makes me forget, I think about her.

21

TODAY
Seven Hours Before

I'm swimming at East Beach with Marnie. We're reaching for the buoy at the same time and she's smiling at me, her eyelashes dripping with ocean water. Her lips taste like salt and watermelon and air and life and everything good in the world. She kicks and swims away and I'm reaching for her, reaching for her reaching for her reaching for her but I can't touch her anymore. I can't get to her.

There was that one last kiss that held everything and nothing all at the same time, and now my arms are not long enough to get to her. My legs aren't strong enough to help me. I'm falling behind. She's pulling away and getting smaller and smaller as she swims out into the ocean without me. The sun is setting and she's disappearing...

Disappearing…

Gone.

I kick and kick and kick, but only one leg moves. I look down. I'm pulling an anchor behind me. I look ahead. Marnie is gone. The sun is gone. All that's left at the buoy are me and the anchor around my ankle, and it's pulling me under. Under the cool ocean where it's quiet.

So quiet.

Bzz. Bzz. Bzz.

The alarm sounds, and I immediately reach for my backpack before I slap the snooze button. I feel the gun still tucked into the front pocket. I pull on my jeans and grab a clean T-shirt from the closet. Grab my hoodie and pat the right pocket. The cell phone is still stashed in there. I pull it out and scroll through the pictures again. Marnie with a one-dimpled smile. Marnie and Ace, kissing. Marnie petting Ace's cat. I close the camera roll and touch the icon for the video folder. I know what I'm going to see. I don't need to watch it again. I touch the trash can icon and delete the video from the phone.

I scratch a note on a Post-It and press it onto the phone: *I know what you did. I will keep her safe.*

I don't say good-bye to my mom before I leave.

I walk right by my truck and right up the driveway and into Ace's driveway. I crouch behind his Jeep and pull the gun from my backpack. I hold it in my hand, still wrapped in the green T-shirt.

Three long, slow breaths from the bottoms of my feet.

I peek around the bumper of the Jeep at Ace's front door. I creep to the driver's side door and put Ace's cell phone with the note on the driver's seat where he can't miss it. I crawl back behind the Jeep and wait. From here, I'll be able to see him come outside. He'll only be twenty-five feet away. I hold the wrapped gun in my lap and breathe.

A few minutes later, I hear a car coming down our street. I creep to the end of Ace's driveway and peek up the road. A silver Honda is coming toward the cul-de-sac.

Marnie's mom. She must be dropping Marnie off at Ace's this morning so they can go to school together.

I fumble with the wrapped gun in my lap and shove it back into the front pocket of my backpack. I can't do it in front of Marnie.

I can't do it in front of anyone else. What if someone else gets in the way?

Everyone else will be safe. Marnie will be safe.

I throw my backpack over my shoulder and run through the sandy yard to my own driveway. I hop in my truck and drive away as quickly as I can.

I look in the rearview mirror just as Marnie gets out of her mom's car and greets Ace with a big hug at the end of his driveway.

22

TODAY
9:35 p.m.

"The plan was to get Ace alone?" Michael asks softly.

I nod, but don't open my eyes.

"You didn't ever plan on going to school this morning, did you?"

I shake my head, still not opening my eyes.

"But when Marnie showed up at Ace's house this morning, you didn't know what else to do with yourself, did you? So you took the gun to school with you," Michael says.

"I want to keep her safe," I say to Michael. I don't recognize my own voice.

"And the only way you can keep Marnie safe is…" Michael begins a sentence and doesn't finish.

"I want to keep her safe," I say again. Michael is just another person who will never understand. There are so many more words in my head than I can't say out loud.

Michael watches me.

"Safe" is the only word I can say. "She needed to be safe."

Michael says nothing. The clock ticks away the seconds, and the pounding in my forehead beats in time with it.

23

TODAY
One Hour Before

Dr. Gunther has left the windows open in the chemistry lab today. He's writing something on the whiteboard, the dry-erase marker squeaking across the surface.

"Can anyone tell me which organs in your body have the highest concentrations of catalase? Anyone?" he asks, not turning around from the whiteboard.

A breeze drifts through, and he's losing us to the hum of bees and the smell of fresh cut grass. I glance at the back of Marnie's head. It keeps dipping slightly, and I know she's struggling to stay awake. I keep my backpack in my lap and my hand over the front pocket. I touch the edges of the lumpy shape in the pocket. The dirty T-shirt hiding my secret.

I glance out the window and remember my father.

He runs the water in the sink and pats at my bloody cheek with a wet towel. "What happened? Did this happen at the park?"

I catch a glimpse of myself in the mirror. Blood is dripping from a small cut under my left eye onto my cheek. My eye is swollen shut and already turning purple above and below my cheekbone.

"Ace popped my basketball," I say before the words get caught in my throat and tears sting my eyes.

"Why did you let him do that?" my dad asks.

I stand up straighter, and the tears stop before they even start. My throat closes, and I stare at my dad in the mirror. His lips turn down and his eyebrows pull in, creasing his forehead.

"I didn't...I didn't let him..." I start to say, but my dad frowns.

"You can't seem weak like that, Sam. That's why he picks at you. He knows you're smaller than he is. I've told you this before," he says, patting at my cheek some more and pulling a Band-Aid from the medicine cabinet.

"But I didn't..."

Dad shakes his head again. "You can't be weak," he repeats.

"Can you do something? Make him stop? Tell his dad?" I say.

Dad shakes his head again. "You've got to stop this yourself, Sam. I can't solve your problems for you anymore. It's not going to help you if your dad steps in every time there's a problem," he says, throwing the towel into the sink.

He walks into the kitchen and stands in front of the freezer, putting ice cubes into a plastic bag. His sigh is loud enough to shake the kitchen walls.

I sink into a chair at the kitchen table, feeling two inches tall. "Are you mad at me?" I ask him.

"Just disappointed," he says, handing me the baggie and going back outside.

Two weeks later, Dad was gone.

I was the one that found him. Lying on the kitchen floor in front of the open refrigerator, a half-gallon of milk spilled around him. An aneurysm, the doctor called it. An artery in his brain just popped, while he stood getting milk for his morning cereal. *Poof* and he was gone. *Poof.*

* * *

The buzzer sounds, and everyone closes their books and reaches for their backpacks.

"Final is just two weeks away, seniors. Keep that in mind," Dr. Gunther says, reaching for the eraser. The class files out the door looking sleepy.

I carry my backpack in front of me, my hand firmly over the front pouch. I feel it there. The pulse of it right beneath the dirty, rolled-up T-shirt. The copper-ended bullets loaded into it so carefully.

Chink. Chink. Chink. Chink. Chink. Chink.

I have six chances to make it right. Six chances to stop being a disappointment.

Six chances to keep Marnie safe. To keep me safe.

But I know I'll only need one. *Poof.*

24

TODAY
9:49 p.m.

I don't feel like I'm breathing anymore. There is a deep pain in my chest and in my gut. My mouth hurts, and I don't think I'll ever be able to open my eyes again.

"Sam? Are you still with me?" Michael says softly.

A sob bubbles up from my throat.

Michaels scoots his chair closer to the bed and puts his hand around my ankle. "I'm right here with you, Sam. You're not doing this alone. Do you think you can keep going?" he asks, his voice barely above a whisper now.

Three deep breaths from the bottoms of my feet. "I can keep going," I say, my voice tight.

"I know this is really hard for you, but can you tell me what happened right before? Anything you can remember, Sam.

People, sounds, anything. Can you see it in your head?"

A deep, black chasm opens in my gut. There's a rope around my middle pulling me down down down. Into the dark. Into the quiet.

Into the peace.

"Sam? Tell me what you see in your head," Michael says.

"I...It's dark," I say, my throat constricting around my words.

"Are you there in the dark, Sam? Who else is there with you?"

"JC almost got in," I say, my voice cracking.

"Almost?"

I hear Michael's pen scratch again.

25

TODAY
Forty-One Minutes Before

I watch Marnie's curls bounce in front of me as she heads toward the cafeteria. The between-class crush in the hallway threatens to push her too far ahead for me to see her, but I'm determined not to lose her. I keep the back of her head in sight all the way there. She sits down at a table with the other cheerleaders, and I know she's safe. For now.

Only then do I find a seat for myself. I'm at JC's table again, and he and Kaplan and the pimple-faced guy ignore me completely. I listen to their conversations with half an ear.

I watch Ace approach Marnie's table from across the cafeteria, my backpack clutched in my lap. I run my index finger over the lump in the front pouch. I'm not going to do it here, in front of everyone. I'll probably have to wait until after school when he's by himself again. No one else in this cafeteria deserves the end I intend to give Ace.

He throws his head back and laughs so loud that it fills the whole cafeteria. Marnie smiles, but the shine in her cheeks never reaches her eyes. Two dimples. She is surrounded by the other cheerleaders and football players, but she has never looked so alone. I want to go to her and tell her that everything's going to be okay. That I'm going to make it right. That I'm going to fix it and she won't have to pretend anymore.

"Earth to Sam?" JC says.

I turn to him.

"Lunch is over," he says.

The cafeteria is clearing out. JC looks at me, and his eyebrows pinch together. He looks like he wants to say something to me. I clutch my backpack tighter and look up at him.

"You okay?" he asks, a delicate tone in his voice.

I look right into his eyes. *I'm about to do this, JC. Please stop me.*

I nod, my backpack a shield between JC and me.

He hesitates a second longer before giving me a sympathetic half-smile and jogging to keep up with Kaplan and the pimple-faced guy.

26

"Why didn't you tell JC when he stopped you in the cafeteria, Sam?" Michael asks.

I open my eyes and let in a little bit of light. I look at the end of my fingers, which seem a hundred miles away on someone else's arm. I flex them and feel nothing.

Michael shifts in his chair and turns a page in his pad. "Sam?"

I turn my head and look at him, my eyes barely open.

"This is when I'm going to need you to tell me everything you remember," he says softly.

I close my eyes again and feel myself slipping far, far away. The pain in my gut is so deep, and I just keep slipping slipping slipping toward it.

Michael touches my ankle and squeezes just a tiny bit. "I'm right here with you. I'm not going to leave you, Sam. It doesn't matter what you say to me, I will not leave you. I'm right here," he says, squeezing again.

I keep my eyes closed and let the tears leak out.

"Do you remember exactly how it happened?" Michael asks.

27

TODAY
12:55 p.m.

He is alone after lunch. The hallway outside of the cafeteria is empty. Ace is directly in front of me, standing outside the bathroom. I stand by the cafeteria doors, watching. The last stragglers are clearing from the long hallway.

He is alone.

He is alone.

I clutch my backpack to my chest and slowly unzip the front pouch. I reach in and let the gun tumble out of the dirty, green Broadmeadow T-shirt wadded up inside. I squeeze my hand around the rubber grip but keep my pointer finger on the trigger. I flip the safety off with my thumb and leave my hand inside my backpack.

"Ace!" I yell, approaching him.

He turns his head, and his expression turns stormy. He reaches into his pocket and pulls out his old cell phone, the yellow Post-It still clinging to the screen. "What the fuck is this about?" he says.

I pull my hand from the bag and stand just a few feet away, gun pointed at his face. Ace stops moving toward me and stands still, his eyes wide and his hands up.

There is a split second, a half-breath, when I feel a tiny niggle of regret.

The heartbeat between the first flex of my index finger and the full squeeze on the trigger. A pause.

Before my eyes can fully blink and the tiny trail of smoke rises up from the exiting bullet, a tick of hesitation.

A twisting in my gut telling me that this is wrong.

That I shouldn't do it.

But by the time my finger eases up on the trigger...

and I know the path of the bullet...

and that pop echoes off the marble floors...

The regret is gone.

The bullet has buried itself in Ace's right knee. He grabs his leg and falls to the floor. He's groaning in agony as I stand over him, gun hanging at my side.

Marnie comes running out of the bathroom and sees Ace lying on the floor, moaning with blood pooling under his leg.

Me. Standing over him with a gun in my hand.

She throws herself on the floor between the nose of my gun

and Ace and looks up at me. "What the hell are you doing?" she yells between sobs.

"Move, Marnie. I'm going to fix it for you. Move," I say quietly.

"Sam...stop. Stop. Don't..." She stands up and puts her hand on the end of the gun.

I try to pull it to me, but she's holding on to it tightly. JC comes around the corner and sees Marnie and I each holding the end of the gun and Ace lying on the floor in a growing puddle of blood.

"Sam! What the hell!" JC says, running toward us.

When Marnie turns around, I pull the gun, hard, out of her hand. She lets go, and I want to aim at Ace again.

"Sam! Stop! Don't!" she yells, and lunges for the gun again.

In the commotion, Ace pulls himself to a sitting position and leans against the wall for support, holding his knee. Blood pours through his fingers.

I am in complete control. I aim at Ace's forehead this time, but Marnie gets in front of me again. I want to push her out of the way, but she's too quick. She has her hand around mine, and we are pulling the gun back and forth between us. JC comes closer and tries to pull my arm down. The three of us are doing some kind of strange waltz in the hallway outside the cafeteria. Each of us has control of the gun and none of us has control of the gun when I hear a loud pop.

28

TODAY
10:17 p.m.

I touch my forehead again, and those fingers that are not mine feel the bumpy stitches. I touch the rest of my face too. Stubble scratches my chin and my cheeks are wet, but I don't feel any more stitches or cuts. Nothing hurts but my forehead.

"You weren't completely in control of the gun when it went off the second time?" Michael says. His voice sounds different.

I open my eyes and look at him.

He looks older somehow. The wrinkles around his eyes have deepened, and purple streaks have appeared right above his cheekbones.

"Hi," he says, managing a very small smile.

I look right at him and blink. My eyes open a little wider.

"What happened after you heard that second pop, Sam?

Who came to find you in that hallway outside the cafeteria?"

"I tried to tell them, Michael," I say.

"I know you did, Sam."

"I didn't..." I say, my voice getting stuck.

Michael touches my wrist. "I'm right here, Sam."

"I just wanted to be safe."

29

TODAY
1:02 p.m.
Six Minutes After

Marnie is screaming. A horrible, gut-wrenching sound is coming from her mouth. The scene swims and unscrambles in front of my eyes. Her hand is bleeding. So much blood. JC is shirtless. His white T-shirt is wrapped around Ace's knee. He's holding Marnie's bleeding hand in one of his hands and pressing his T-shirt to Ace's knee with the other hand. He looks at me, his eyes wild and scared.

"What did you do! What did you do!" he screams across the hall at me. It's not a question.

I stand still, the gun hanging at my side. *What did I do? What did I do?* There's blood, and it's not just Ace's. Marnie. Marnie's bleeding, and that's not what was supposed to happen. Marnie is hurt. And I'm holding a gun to my side.

"You did this! You did this!" Marnie screams at me. "You did this, you sick fuck!"

I did this. I did this. The blood on the floor. The blood on Marnie and Ace. JC in the middle of it all.

I did this.

The barrel of the gun is warm against my temple.

I can hear the frantic *fwump-fwump-fwump* of my heart slamming against my ribs in the chaotic hallway.

A tiny voice inside is fighting its way up my throat. *No. No, no, no*, it's saying. The sound never makes it past my teeth.

There are loud, quick footfalls echoing through the marble hallway.

The sun streams through the thick-paned windows and glints off the trophy case, throwing golden stripes of light across the green lockers.

Ace's breathing is labored. His eyes wide and wild.

I sink to the floor.

Darkness.

With my back against a locker, I bring the gun to my forehead again and again and again, harder and harder each time. Every hit slows the thrumming in my brain. Holding the gun to my temple helps too. So quiet. So dark. The steel is still warm, and I press it hard against the soft spot. I close my eyes and count. Two bullets are gone. Four are left. But I'll only need one.

"Stop! Stop it! Sam, no!" JC screams across the hallway. His sneakered feet make muted flapping sounds on the marble floor, and he is in my lap in a flash. He pulls the gun away from my head. I don't fight him.

"Stop," he says almost silently. "Stop."

I let the gun fall into my lap, and I look at JC's face. He's crying.

The warmth spreads slowly from my toes to my chest, where it wells up like a dam before finally breaking and escaping my lungs in big, gasping sobs. I see JC's face in front of me, just inches from my own.

"I'm not a disappointment," I say to JC's face.

"You're okay, buddy. You're okay," he keeps repeating. He's inhaling but not exhaling. His eyes dart all over, like a trapped animal.

The tears come, and I can't stop them. "I'm not a disappointment. I'm not a disappointment...I'm not...I'm not..." I say between sobs.

JC looks right into my face.

"Make it stop, JC."

"You're okay, buddy."

Mr. Patton is the first one here. I hear his shoes in the hallway before I see him round the corner. He stops short at the top of the hallway, his eyebrows creeping up his forehead as he takes in the scene. Ace and Marnie are closest to him, blood pooling around them. Ten or fifteen bloody sneaker prints between the two of them and JC and me. JC straddling my lap with my face in his hands. Me. Sitting with a gun in my lap.

"I tried to tell you," I say, pointing my finger at Mr. Patton. I don't think he hears me.

He goes to Ace and Marnie first, pulling his radio out of his back pocket. "I'm going to need some help outside the cafeteria. Get everyone out of the building," he says into the radio. There's a sense of urgency in his voice, a shaky quality I've never heard before.

I blink and there are more people. JC is not in my lap anymore.

I blink and there is a cop.

Breen, his shiny name tag says.

"You're going to have to stand up now, son," Breen says, his bald head reflecting the harsh fluorescent hallway lights. I glance to the side. More uniformed people are hovering over Marnie and Ace. Marnie is crying loudly, a strangled sound coming from her throat. JC is talking to another uniform. He isn't wearing a shirt, but the front of his body is covered with blood. Not his own.

I look down at my lap. The gun isn't in my hand anymore, but my fingers are still bent around an invisible trigger.

I blink and I'm in the back of Breen's police car. "You're going to the hospital, Sam," he says.

I blink and there are kids with their hands over their mouths, huddled together in groups outside the school. The ambulance lights spin and throw red light across their faces.

30

TODAY
2:19 p.m.
One Hour and
Twenty-Two Minutes After

A nurse adjusts the IV pole and checks my arm. Her fingers are warm.

I try to reach up and scratch my nose with my right hand. My left hand is attached to it with a plastic restraint. Both hands touch my nose. My ankles are attached to the metal bed frame.

"Someone will be in to talk with you in a few minutes," the nurse says, giving me a tight-lipped smile. "His name is Michael."

"JC," I say. "Is he okay? Marnie?"

She looks down at the floor. "I'm sorry I can't give you any information."

She leaves the room with her bucket of medicine and

needles. When she opens the door, I see Breen standing out-side. He nods at me, folding his arms across his chest.

A man with a green tie comes through the door and closes it behind him again. He is carrying a weathered leather brief-case, and a gold pen is tucked into his shirt pocket. He settles his tall frame into the chair with the wooden arms. He pulls it closer to the bed and spends a minute or two adjusting his pant legs and running his fingers between his shirt collar and the loose skin on his neck. He pulls a small recorder from the briefcase, as well as a yellow legal pad. He scratches something at the top of the pad with his gold pen without looking at me.

I stare down at my hands. The cuts left by the restraints are tiny and straight. I touch the one on my right hand. It stings a little bit, but stops when I let go. I touch it a few more times.

"How did a kid like you end up here?" the guy with the tie asks.

31

NOVEMBER
Six Months After

It will be Thanksgiving soon. Paper turkeys made from brown construction paper handprints and brightly colored paper feathers line the dingy windows of the common room. I try not to talk to anyone when I'm out here. They try to talk to me, though.

"What did you do?"

"Why are you in here?"

"You're awfully tall. How old are you, anyway?"

Everyone wants to know. Kids with tattoos on their necks. Kids with glasses and braces. Kids with scarred knuckles and shifty eyes. Kids that look like they should be reading Harry Potter novels at night with a flashlight and eating dinner with Mom and Dad. They all want to know.

Michael visits five times a week. I talk to him. He says it's okay if I don't want to interact with anyone here. Juvie. It's only for six months, he said. Then...we'll see, he said.

Today is the day of "we'll see." Turns out "we'll see" means I can go home. "We'll see" is community service, living with Mom and Grandpa, and weekly visits with Michael.

"Sam?" a guard approaches. "They're ready for you now," he says.

* * *

The air is thinner beyond the gates. Not musty with sweat and tears and blood and regret. I take a deep swallow of it and let it reach down my throat, through my lungs, and all the way to my feet. I turn my face to the setting sun and swim in it.

Mom and Grandpa are waiting. They smile, tight-lipped, when they see me carrying a plastic bag of my things, knuckles white. Mom grabs for Grandpa's hand, and he squeezes it tightly. I see all of this unfold as I walk down the sidewalk toward them.

"Ready to go home, Sam?" Grandpa asks, his voice even and low.

I nod.

My mother says nothing to me, but puts her hand on my shoulder briefly as I fold my legs into the backseat of Grandpa's truck. No one talks during the twenty-minute ride home either. My ears ring.

Mom unlocks the door, and she and Grandpa go inside first. I pause on the front porch and look toward Ace's house. A For

Sale sign sways in the November breeze. Leaves and pine needles gather on the lawn and driveway. The house looks cold. Forgotten. Michael told me about this. To expect to see Ace's house either empty or with a new family inside. It still doesn't prepare me for what it feels like to look over there. Numb.

Inside my own house, everything is just how it was when I left that morning in May, and yet everything is different. The furniture is in the same place, the pillows and curtains are still the same, and even the smells are the same. But something is missing. It takes me a minute to realize what it is, but once I do, it's like a boot to my chest.

Me. I'm what's missing.

There are no more basketball trophies on the bookcase in the living room. My senior picture is gone from the mantel. The frame Mom bought to hold my high school diploma is on the floor by the fireplace, empty. It never did see a diploma. I blink a few times before walking down the hall toward the steps to my room.

It's spotless, and there are new curtains on the window. My basketball trophies are here, on shelves that line the walls near the ceiling. My senior picture is here too. There are several new pairs of jeans folded on the bed, as well as a stack of brightly colored T-shirts. A sport coat hangs in plastic wrap on the closet door. I walk to it and finger the plastic.

"For college interviews," Grandpa says from behind me. "When you're ready," he adds.

I turn and nod at him, looking at the floor. I sit down on the bed, and Grandpa sits next to me.

"I understand it will take awhile, Sam, but you'll get your feet under you," he says.

I don't know if I believe him. The thought of staying here in Easthaven, where almost everyone hates me, is terrifying. Michael worked with the courts to make sure I had a lighter sentence because of the bullying I had put up with for years, but to most of Easthaven, I am still "that kid who shot the Broadmeadow quarterback."

"You'll start your last semester at Gadsden High in January and finally get that diploma. You can apply to schools again. It's going to turn out okay, Sam," Grandpa says.

"Gadsden," I say, staring at the floor.

"It's just one semester that you have to make up. Your grades were excellent before...well, before. You're lucky the school board is letting you go to Gadsden. You've got to stand on your own two feet," he says, patting my knee and standing up.

I watch him walk away from my room, and my stomach lurches. High school. Again. I know I will be able to get through it with Michael's help, but I'm nervous anyway. Michael says to put one foot in front of the other, and pretty soon you will have walked a mile. He's already talked to the guidance counselor at Gadsden and set up daily meetings with her for me.

The house phone rings, and I look at the caller ID on my desk and smile.

"Hello, Mrs. Cushman," I say, picking up the receiver.

"Oh, my honey bun! I have missed you so much! How are you?" she shouts into the phone. I have to pull it away from my ear, but I smile.

"I missed you too, Mrs. C," I say.

"Dinner at our house tonight, Sammy. I won't take no for an answer. Jay Jay is coming home for his Thanksgiving break, and he can't wait to see you," she says, barely taking a breath. "Seven o'clock. We'll set a place for you."

I go back downstairs, touching the walls as I walk. I want there to be some kind of memory attached to them. Some kind of spark that makes me think of the good things that happened to me here. I feel nothing.

Downstairs, Mom is in the sunroom, stretching. I look out the window. Grandpa's truck is gone. I stand in the doorway of the sunroom, watching Mom.

"Where'd Grandpa go?" I ask.

"He had a meeting at the school," she answers, her eyes closed as she stretches her hands toward her toes.

"Oh," I answer.

Suddenly I feel like I don't belong there. I have a sinking realization that the house was plenty full before I came back home, and now there's another body here that doesn't belong. The odd man out. The awkward puzzle piece that doesn't quite fit into the empty hole.

"I'm really sorry..." I start to say.

She holds her hand up to me, but doesn't turn my way or open her eyes.

"Don't do this," she says. "Not now."

I sit down on the soft rug in the sunroom and try to mimic my mother's movements. Three deep breaths from the bottoms of my feet. Hands in my lap, palms up. She still doesn't open her eyes.

"Your record will be sealed on your eighteenth birthday," she says, her voice cracking.

"I know," I say. "Just two more weeks."

"You'll finish your last semester at Gadsden High and start all over again. Apply to schools. Get a job. Everything is going to be fine," she says, exhaling.

"I know, Mom. I know how lucky I am that I can start to put this behind me. I don't know that I would have been this lucky without Michael," I say. I stare at her, but she never opens her eyes. I don't think she's talking to me. I think she's talking to herself.

"This will not define us," she says.

Us?

I stand up from the floor and walk out of the sunroom. "I'm going to JC's for dinner," I say over my shoulder as I walk out the door.

I walk to JC's house, my heavy coat wrapped around me. I have a strange churning in my gut. Neither Mom nor Grandpa really seemed that excited to have me home. Everything feels completely off. It's almost like Mom wants to pretend it never happened. I can't do that.

It happened. It happened to me. It happened because of me.

There is a beat-up gray Honda in JC's driveway with about a half dozen UConn bumper stickers on it. I smile. He's already home.

JC opens the door as I'm walking up the winding sidewalk. He comes running out, grabs my shoulders, and pulls me into a giant bear hug before I even make it to the front stoop.

"Oh my God, Sam!" he says into my neck. His shoulders shake, but he doesn't let go.

I pat his back and try to return the hug. He lets go and ushers me into his living room, closing the door behind us.

"Look what I found outside!" JC yells.

"There he is!" Mrs. Cushman comes to the front door, wiping her hands on a dish towel. She throws it over her shoulder and pulls me into a hug.

"I've missed you so much," she says. "Did you get my letters?"

"Every one of them," I say, and I mean it. Mrs. C wrote me at least twice a week the entire six months I was in juvie. Nothing real deep, but long letters. Handwritten words of encouragement, short snippets about what JC was up to, sometimes pictures of the projects Mr. C was working on. I read every single one of them at least three times. I wrote her back too.

She smiles and squeezes me around the shoulders. "You and JC go catch up. Dinner will be in a little bit," she says.

JC motions outside. He tucks his basketball under his arm, and we walk down the road to the playground court we went to when we were kids. The sun is setting, and the wind is howling. We are the only people at the playground.

JC starts shooting and grabbing his own rebounds. I hover near the bench, not sure whether to sit down and watch or just stand here. JC sends me a perfect bounce pass. "Shoot," he says, nodding toward the hoop.

I dribble toward the basket, and it feels weird. My muscles are tight, and the ball scrapes my hand and feels too something. Too big. Too small. Too much.

I bounce the ball back to JC. "How's school?" I ask.

"Awesome," he says. "Did you get my letters too?"

"I did," I say. JC sent a few postcards from UConn. Short notes of the "thinking about ya" variety. I hung them up on my wall with gum. I tell him this.

He smiles at his shoes. "What do you think about going to Gadsden?" he asks, shooting a three-pointer and making it easily.

I just shrug and sit down on the bench, my hands in my pockets.

"It'll work out, Sam. It's just a little detour," he says, sitting down next to me on the bench.

I nod and look at my feet. My gut is churning again. I

thought it would feel okay to be with JC. I thought it would be easy.

"The Quinns moved out of state," he says, dribbling the ball between his knees.

I nod again.

"Ace is still here, though. At Oceanside," he says, getting up and taking a few shots from the foul line.

I hold my breath and wait for the news to sink in. I squeeze my fists in my coat pocket and wonder what I'm supposed to feel. All I feel is numb.

"He had to do a bunch of community service, you know. He was scrubbing graffiti off the playground equipment at the public beach for a few weeks. Then someone said they saw him hauling canned goods for the soup kitchen right before he started school." JC takes another shot from the foul line.

"Community service, huh?" I scuff my foot in the loose gravel under the bench. My stomach turns.

"Yeah. He lost his scholarship because of the...um." JC stops dribbling and looks at my face. "You don't want to hear about all of this, do you?"

I shake my head. "Not really, no."

He dribbles from one end of the court to the other and makes a nice easy lay-up.

"I talked to Marnie a few days ago," he says.

I sit up a little straighter. "She okay?"

"She's good," he says.

I want to know more, but I don't feel like I can ask.

"She went to Florida State, you know," he says.

I exhale. Florida State. That's 1,300 miles from Oceanside. One thousand, three hundred miles between her and Ace.

JC hands me the ball, and I dribble between my knees while I sit on the bench. It doesn't feel as weird as it did. I get into a rhythm and stand up, not stopping my dribble. I walk toward the goal and take a shot. I miss by a lot. I bounce the ball back to JC. He shoots a foul shot and makes it.

"We better go home. Almost dinnertime," he says.

I follow him away from the playground, casting one last glance toward the rusting hoops.

The table is set with dark-blue linens, and white candles are burning when we walk back into the house. A pot roast is in the middle of the table, with small bowls of vegetables dotted around it.

"This is wonderful, Mrs. C, but you didn't have to go to all this trouble," I say when we're all seated.

"Our days of TV trays are over, Sammy. It's no trouble. Plus, our boys are home! There's nothing more worth celebrating than that," she says.

Her boys. I feel my cheeks burn, and I have to look away. I don't feel like an awkward puzzle piece.

The Cushmans keep up a lively conversation during dinner, and I don't have to say many words at all. No one comments that I'm being too quiet. Mrs. Cushman serves me more mashed potatoes when I finish mine, and Mr. Cushman fills my water glass every time I take a sip. JC talks about all of his classes and how much studying he thinks he's going to have to do to get through his finals next month.

Everything feels warm. For the first time in a long time, I smile and laugh without thinking. When dinner is over, I help clean up. JC is putting the last plate into the cupboard when the kitchen falls silent. I can feel all kinds of things start to bubble up in that silence.

"I really should be going back home," I say quietly.

Mrs. Cushman smiles softly. She and her husband walk me to the door.

"It's good to have you home, Sam. Don't be a stranger. Our door is always open," Mr. C says, patting me on the back.

Mrs. C hugs me and rocks back and forth for a good minute.

"I'll walk with you," JC says, pulling on his heavy coat and tucking his basketball under his arm.

We walk a full block without speaking. My stomach isn't churning anymore, and the silence feels okay.

"Feel like hanging out tomorrow?" JC finally says when we get to the top of my street.

"Sure," I say, not really sure at all. Hanging out. It was something JC and I did all the time before. It was effortless. But now, I don't even know what hanging out means. Nothing feels like it fits. Words I used to understand now have a completely different meaning. Michael said it would take awhile before things started to feel somewhat normal. And it would never be like it was before. Before. Is that what my life is going to be now? Separated into before and after?

We walk down my street until we reach the top of my driveway. I look over at Ace's house. The driveway is empty, and there is a Realtor's lockbox on the front door. JC shuffles his feet in the sandy gravel at the curb.

"Remember what you said to me that day?" he asks.

I shake my head. I only remember bits and pieces of that day. And the bits and pieces show up at random times too. While I'm brushing my teeth. Eating the Tuesday oatmeal breakfast. Changing my sheets.

"What did I say?" I ask.

"It's not important," JC says. "It's not true anyway."

He claps me on the shoulder before turning and running back down the street toward his house. He dribbles the basketball the whole way. I watch him until he reaches the stop sign at the end of my street and turns left. Even when he's gone, I can still hear the echo of his dribbling from the top of my driveway.

I turn and look toward my house. The lights are on in the living room, and I can see Grandpa in the rocking chair, the newspaper spread across his lap. He catches sight of me standing in the pool of streetlight. He nods and waves without smiling. I nod and wave back. Michael's words bounce around in my head: It's going to take some time.

32

JANUARY
Eight Months After

Sometimes when it's real quiet at night, I think about Marnie. How things happened. How much I miss the person she was. How much I miss the person I was when we were together.

Sometimes I wonder what life would have been like if I hadn't gone to school with a gun that day. Ace and I would have been at Oceanside College together. That's usually where I stop wondering and remind myself that I *did* go to school with a gun that day. No amount of wishing or hoping or wondering will change that.

Sometimes there's shit you just can't take back. Wondering how life would be different if I had made a different choice is one of those things Michael calls "an epic waste of a time."

I start the second semester of my senior year at Gadsden

High School tomorrow. I worry that it will feel too much like Broadmeadow. I worry that people will want to talk to me about what happened with Ace. I worry that people will look at me and only see that one gigantic mistake. I worry that I will have no friends. I worry that I will have friends but they won't be anything like JC.

I have an appointment with Michael tonight.

"You ready for your big day tomorrow?" he says, kicking his feet up onto the arm of the couch I am sitting on. He leans back in his spinny chair.

"I think so," I say, trying my best to swallow every bit of worry that has been sticking to my ribs since November.

"It's okay if you're not, you know. It's not going to be easy," he says.

I nod, but I can feel that swallowed worry trying to climb back up. Clawing its way from my throat to the back of my tongue.

"I don't expect that everything's going to go perfectly, Sam. You'll probably have a few hiccups. I need you to anticipate that," he says. "You have my number in your phone. I've already spoken with your new guidance counselor, Ms. Waller. She's expecting you tomorrow morning."

"Okay," I say, the anxiety building in my gut. I know my appointment with Michael is almost over. I'll be one step closer to starting over. High school. The belly of the beast.

"You can do this, you know," he says, standing up and clapping me on the shoulder.

"I know," I say, even though I'm not completely convinced.

The next day, I'm up before the sun rises. I put on jeans and a green sweater. I leave my black hoodie hanging in the closet.

Grandpa drives me to Gadsden High School on his way to Broadmeadow. He doesn't say much and keeps the heat vent on full blast for the entire ride.

A handful of rocks starts to tumble in my gut. "I'm sorry you have to bring me to school, Grandpa," I say.

At first, Grandpa says nothing, only grunts a little bit. More like a quiet *humph* than any meaningful noise. As we pull into the circular driveway in front of Gadsden, he turns the heat down a few notches.

"Sammy," he says finally, his voice a low rumble.

"Yeah, Grandpa?"

"You've got nothing to apologize for," he says, not taking his eyes off the slow-moving traffic in front of him.

I don't answer.

"You're standing on your own two feet. That's all anyone can ask of a man," he says, putting his truck in park at the front door and letting the engine idle.

"Yes, sir."

"I'm proud of you. I know it can't be easy to start over like this. Your dad would be proud of you too," he says to his lap.

I don't move from the seat. I grip the strap of my backpack in my lap and search my head for the right words.

"No one is disappointed, Sammy," he says, turning the heater up full blast again and putting the truck in drive.

I climb out of the truck, the last dregs of fear and worry seeping from my fingertips. I watch Grandpa drive away from me, and I take a deep breath of cold January air.

I open the door to the school, and a fresh blast of warm air greets me. No one notices. No one looks at me and stares. No one points or whispers.

I'm not just the broken kid who shot the Broadmeadow quarterback. I'm no longer the silent boy that pulled his black hoodie around his head and disappeared from reality. I'm not the scared kid that was afraid to ask for help. I'm not a disappointment.

"Excuse me, can you tell me where to find Ms. Waller?" I ask a kid walking near me.

"Right in there." He points to his left. "You new here?"

"Yeah, I am," I say.

"I'm Raj," he says, sticking his hand out.

I hesitate for just a minute. "Sam," I say, shaking Raj's hand.

He blinks and stares at my face for a beat longer than necessary. "Welcome to Gadsden," he says.

RESOURCES

If you're being bullied, or if you have thoughts of harming yourself or someone else, help is out there.

The website www.teensagainstbullying.org has extensive information and support for those who are bullied or witness bullying.

Need someone to talk to? The following resources offer free and confidential twenty-four-hour assistance:

- **121help.me** Call 1-855-201-2121 or text HELP to 20121. www.121help.me
- **Crisis Text Line** Text START to 741-741. Website also includes listings for live chat with other support organizations. www.crisistextline.org
- **National Suicide Prevention Lifeline** Call 1-800-273-TALK (8255). www.suicidepreventionlifeline.org

ACKNOWLEDGMENTS

Without the tireless efforts of many, Sam, Ace, and Marnie would still be sitting in an untouched folder on my laptop. Several people deserve boisterous applause for the role they played in helping me share Sam's story.

To my editor, Wendy McClure: Your insight and gentle guidance took this story to places I never dreamed it could go. Thank you for believing in me and in Sam's voice.

To the team at Albert Whitman: Thank you for the little fixes (and the not-so-little fixes) and for bringing this book to life.

To my agent, Courtney Miller-Callihan: Thank you for having my back. Thank you for always saying "Yeah! Try that!" whenever I called to say, "I have this really screwy idea…" Thank you for knowing I could get here. Thank you for bridges and hot tubs and endless text chats. Thank you for being you.

To Ash Parsons and Vicky Shecter: Your unwavering encouragement—coupled with *Friday Night Lights* references and shirtless, cute guy GIFs—carried me through many a dark moment. I love you both. TUDlife fist bump.

To the DSDs: Lauren Karcz, Ashleigh Hally, and Cathi O'Tyson, you've been with me on this journey since day one. There's no way I could ever have gotten to this point without all of you.

To Cathy C. Hall and Doraine Bennett: The universe put you in my path for a reason. Your enthusiasm and friendship pulled me through many a thorny plot problem! I will forever be grateful.

To Suzanne Waller: You've shown me how to be brave. There is no greater lesson than this. You're always in my heart.

To Mom, Dad, and Kristen: My very first cheering section! Thank you for never saying I couldn't, shouldn't, or wouldn't. I love you.

To Ryan and Lauren: Look! I did it! Thank you for your patience and understanding throughout my endless dinner chats about people that only exist in my head. You are the best things to ever happen to me, and you make me so proud every day.

To Steve: You knew. You always knew. You're my cheerleader, my BS-meter, my idea machine, and my best friend. For all of these reasons and a million more, I'm forever grateful. Love you to the moon and back.

Finally, to Gram and Gramps: I hope I've made you proud. I miss you both every single day.

ABOUT THE AUTHOR

Kara Bietz lives with her husband and their two children near Houston, Texas, where she works in a high school library. She spends her evenings dictating story ideas to her dogs, jotting down plots, character arcs, and story lines on a giant whiteboard, and eventually turning those conversations and notes into manuscripts. This is her first novel.

weee!